Our Infinite Depths

ISBN: 978-1-9991282-6-5

Chapter 1

I've been dreading this day all summer. Jayden is leaving tomorrow, and I have no idea when I'll see him again. For all I know, the answer is *never*.

Jayden lifts his head off mine. "I have to go home," he says.

"Five more minutes."

"I can't."

"Please."

He removes his arm from around my shoulders. His eyes are his best features, though to most people they're almost too dark to be human. When they settle on me, disappointment wells up in my chest—ice-cold and bitter, like lemonade without the sugar.

"You're going to miss me too much," he whispers. "Promise me you won't let it tear you apart."

"I can't promise anything."

"You've been able to keep every other promise."

"Jayden—" The words stick in my throat, and I pick some lint off my jeans instead.

"It's okay. You don't have to say anything."

So I don't.

He sighs and rises from the porch steps. His hand slips through my fingers until only the memory of his skin remains.

"I'll text you in the morning," Jayden promises, sticking his hands in his front pockets. "I'm leaving early."

"How early?"

"Around five."

That's only ten hours from now. A blink, and he's gone.

"And I'll call you when I arrive in Kingston. I'll give you my schedule then." When I don't speak, he adds, "This is really important to me, Gabby. It's my future—probably the only one I'll ever have."

"But it's the military," I protest, hating the way my voice shakes, "it's—"

"I know." Jayden pulls me into his embrace. His denim jacket is engulfed in a cloud of Axe—a smell I instinctively register as Jayden, even when someone else is wearing it. Mom says it makes him too predictable, but I'm pretty sure joining the military is the total opposite of safe and secure.

He lifts my chin. "I love you."

"Okay."

"Okay?"

"I love you, too."

"But…"

I pull away from him. "This sounds like the end."

"It's not the end. Think of it as an intermission. Look, my mom wants me to be home before ten." His lips skim my forehead. Before I know it, he's getting into his truck, turning it on, and driving out of my life, leaving two deep grooves in the gravel.

There are two kinds of guys in this world: guys who look like trouble, but aren't, and guys who look like they could be the perfect boyfriend, only to destroy your life the first chance they get. When I met Jayden, he was firmly in the first camp. I'd been serving nachos at the local arena when he swaggered up to the counter with his coal-black eyes and jeans jacket, leaving his friends to their idiotic jokes and obnoxious laughter in the background.

"Can I get some nachos?" he asked, giving me a whiff of Axe as he leaned in close.

I crossed my arms. "I don't know. Can you?"

Jayden smiled, impervious to my attitude. "*May* I get some nachos," he said, and that's when I really started to pay attention to his eyes, like how you only notice the beauty of a sunrise on the second glance.

I fetched a boat and filled it with chips, then held it under the pump that dispensed the cheese. It was weird to think about a guy as having beautiful eyes, but that was the only way to describe them. Jayden was stunning, like Edward in *Twilight*. Which meant he was probably dangerous, too.

"Do you always add this much cheese?" he asked.

I snapped into focus; the nachos were fully submerged in a lake of cheddar-flavoured lava, so I set the boat on the counter and rang up his order. Anything to avoid looking at his too-gorgeous-to-be-human face.

"Thanks." Jayden paid for his nachos and began to walk away, only to return a second later. "Can I ask you for one more thing?"

I automatically handed him a wad of napkins, but he shook his head.

"Actually, I was going to ask what you're doing on Saturday," Jayden said.

"Oh." The arena was filling up with people. Most of them were lining up to get nachos, but Jayden didn't notice. Or care.

After an eternity, I stuttered, "I'm working."

"Cool. By the way, how old are you?"

"Fifteen."

Jayden smiled and slid away from the counter, freeing up space for the next person. "My uncle has a fish and chips place down by the lake. I swear you'll be hooked from the first bite."

He ended up taking the napkins. I hadn't been prepared for him to steal my heart.

✳

Jayden was the perfect boyfriend. He was older, sophisticated, and had a car, which came in handy for driving me to the mall and work. He was on a first-name basis with the teachers and hung out with the other seniors in the parking lot at lunch. Everyone loved Jayden—everyone, that was, but my parents.

It wasn't just that Jayden was two years older than me. It was that Jayden treated high school like one long intermission: he always seemed to be figuring stuff out, or exploring his options, but struggled to commit to anything resembling real responsibility. Dad claimed his life "lacked structure." Mom made me go on birth control, even though Jayden and I hadn't even talked about sex, much less marriage and babies. But sometimes, the people who seem perfect on paper are the ones who need the most editing. Jayden was a crumpled up page I kept smoothing down, over and over again, until I'd memorized every crease; until he eventually fell apart in my hands.

I should have known something was wrong when I walked in on him Googling basic cadet training. The words meant nothing to me at the time, other than that I'd have to pry him away from the computer and beg for attention.

"What are you looking at?" I asked him. I was sprawled out on my bed. Jayden was sitting at my desk, and his eyes were glassy and unfocused, very un-Edward-like.

That was when he started crying.

Jayden told me all kinds of things that day: the trouble he was in at school for missing class, how the principal had found drugs in his locker, how his uncle had fired him for giving food away to his friends. His head was heavy in my lap, like a bowling ball covered in thick, bronze hair. He sounded so scared and lost. And the worst part was, I didn't know what to say.

When he eventually stopped crying, Jayden said, "Maybe I'll join the military."

I ceased stroking his hair. "The military?"

Jayden nodded. He was staring out the window at our barn and the dust devils that kept spinning across the driveway. "I need structure."

I was suddenly furious at my father for planting that idea in his mind. Jayden didn't need structure—he needed me. Or at least I thought he did.

"You can't join the military," I argued, "you just can't. You can't."

"I have to," he whispered, and the room became eerily silent.

Jayden was joining the military. Once that thought took hold, it started to spread and multiply. I was trapped on a frozen pond of possibilities, watching the ice crack beneath my feet. Deep down, I knew he was right: He needed structure. He needed purpose. But I needed something else, and I didn't know what that thing was until it started to slip away.

"What if you get sent to war?" I asked.

The wind whipped up another spiral of sand. "Then I guess I'll have to fight."

"Jayden—"

"Don't cry, Gabby." He turned onto his back and raised a hand to my cheek. His eyes lit up, dazzling and utterly haunted. "I'll always protect you."

*

Three days until school starts.

I've been lying in bed since yesterday afternoon, my sinuses all achy and swollen. Just when I think I'm done crying, Jayden pops into my head with his big, beautiful eyes, and the cycle begins again.

The heavy tread of my father's footsteps interrupts my mid-afternoon pity party. My bedroom is located in the attic; the stairs leading up to it are old and creaky, although I've learned which spots to avoid if I want to sneak out. Dad appears at the foot of my bed wearing a faded green shirt, dust-caked overalls, and boots up to his knees. A fringe of grey hair skirts his muddy ballcap.

"It's a beautiful day," he says. "You should be outside."

"I'm sick," I say automatically.

"Because you spend too much time inside."

I turn on my opposite side and end up staring at a picture of Jayden, shirtless and glistening, on the beach in Cobourg. His Ray-Bans hide his gorgeous eyes, but not his smile.

After a minute, dad says, "Do you want to hear a joke?"

"No."

"What's black, white, and red all over?"

"I don't know. Don't care."

"A dairy farm that's losing money."

Dad is the king of unfunny jokes. This one's so bad, I almost want to cry, except I can't because I'm all cried out over Jayden.

Dad eventually leaves me alone. He's right: it *is* a beautiful day outside. The sun is slanting through my window in sheets, gilding the particles of dust that cross its path. August heat lingers in the air. I stick out my hand and feel the sun's rays collide with my skin. Jayden must be settled in by now. I check my phone, but there's nothing new to see. No texts or missed calls. Just the time, moving forward minute by minute.

Outside, the air is even hotter. The weather forecast has been promising rain for a week, and today, we may just get it: the sky is steely with clouds. Dad has opened the doors at both ends of the barn to encourage a breeze. It's business as usual down here, with the cows ruminating in the field and the papers rustling in dad's office.

My parents bought the farm when my brother and I were young. Mom grew up in the country and wanted more than anything for us to have the same carefree childhood she did, before people got paranoid about kids playing in the streets or drinking water from a hose. Dad was tired of taking orders and wanted to work for himself. So, one summer we packed up our comfortable suburban life and moved to a small town in rural Ontario, far away from our friends, family, and unnecessary human interaction.

It took a few years for dad to get the hang of being a farmer, and a few more years for us to turn a steady profit. By then, I was in high school and ready to abandon my idyllic childhood for more scintillating activities, like making out with Jayden. In fact, it was only when he announced his plan to join the military that I began to see our farm as a shrine to our humble beginnings, and the place where everything (not just the livestock) was still black and white. Then the farmland adjacent to ours got bought up by some construction company and turned into a bunch of cookie-cutter houses. More people should equate to a greater demand for milk, but it seems like everyone is going dairy-free these days, so good luck to us, I guess.

I mope around the barn for a bit, looking for something to do. Eventually, desperate for some relief from the heat, I uncoil the hose and haul it out to the water troughs for a refill. The water gushing from the nozzle is crystal-clear and ice-cold. As I'm letting the water splash across my wrists, mom emerges from the barn and walks toward me with her hands in her pockets. She's wearing Mom-jeans and a yellow top with a ruffled neckline, and her hair hangs in a disheveled braid down her back.

"It's nice to see you out of the house, for a change," mom says, her face flushed. "Any word from Jayden?"

"Not yet. I'm sure he's just busy though." The trough is nearly full, but I'm still sweltering, so I keep watering my arms as if they might suddenly sprout a vegetable garden.

Mom folds her arms. "Gabby, we need to talk."

"About what?"

"I know you're disappointed about Jayden, but I think this will be good for him. It was time for him to plant his roots somewhere."

I consider telling her that the military doesn't guarantee a bright future, but go on filling the troughs instead.

"And you never know—maybe one day, when you're both older and have careers, you'll find your way back to each other—"

"Sure—if he doesn't get blown up first."

"Gabby."

"What do you want me to say? That I'm happy for him?"

"There are lots of jobs in the Forces that don't involve active combat," mom says in a conciliatory tone. "And even if he does decide to go that route, you should be happy that he found something to do with his life. Serving one's country is an incredible honour."

"He shouldn't be serving his country! He should be here with me, where he's safe."

"You can't force people to stay. When it's their time to go…" Mom doesn't finish her thought out loud. But it's too late: my face is already damp with tears. I drop the open end of the hose on the ground and head toward the driveway to continue my pity party in peace. This wasn't how I pictured the summer ending. How I pictured Jayden and me ending. Deep down, I knew we weren't meant to last—if not for the difference in our ages, then the inevitable divergence in our lives once I headed off to college to pursue a career as a fitness instructor. Jayden never fully understood my choices, but he always supported them… yet I can't bring myself to reciprocate.

As my feet hit the gravel of our driveway, my anger over Jayden's leaving fades to a lazy hum at the back of my mind. Our farm sits at the back of the lot, and during the summer, when the trees are fullest, it becomes practically invisible from the road. The summer heat is building into a voluptuous storm cloud—darkness in the middle of the day.

Then the rain starts. Somewhere out there, Jayden is settling in to his new life at the Royal Military College. I wonder if they'll make him shave off his glorious curls. Not that it matters: to me, his beauty is immortal.

The path leading back to the house is long and matted with clumps of leaves. I count 187 paces from the fence to the front door, where I find my family seated around the kitchen table.

"Gabby," dad says, "you're just in time. Come join us."

I pull off my boots and absently pour myself a glass of pop. Mom is gabbing to Rick, the haggard old potato farmer with tanned skin and a perpetual scowl, whose lot abuts ours to the north.

"Of course, Gabby loves the new fitness complex. Can't drag her home once we're there," mom gushes, helping herself to a cookie from the plate in the centre of the table.

Rick grunts. "I guess that's the type of thing you'd expect from a girl," he says. "The whole city scene and whatnot."

Mom asks, "Can I get you some more coffee, Rick?"

"Thank you, but no." He drains the mug and sets it aside. "Bev, I know you have a lot to think about—as we all do, especially with all the construction going on lately—but I need your help. I got this nephew—great kid, good head on his shoulders and all that. Anyway, he's going to be moving to town for a while and wants to get some work experience while he's here. I already have four boys of my own, as you know, and Sharon and I don't have any extra room. I told my sister I'd talk to you and Gus… in case you were looking to hire some help."

Mom nods. "Well, of course, we'd be happy to have the help. There's plenty of room in the attic for another bed. Gabby could use the company anyway, right hon?"

I nearly choke on a cookie when I hear this.

"It's only for a little while," Rick says. "Just until he saves up money for school. Vince is a good kid, as I said, but I should probably mention—"

"Dad, I caught a creepy-crawler!" Ryan bursts into the room with an insect net and a jar half-filled with decaying leaves. He rattles it wildly as dad shoos him outside.

"A lovely specimen," dad says, referring to the black-and-brown caterpillar rolling around in the glass container. "Why don't you take your little friend to play outside?"

Ryan sulks out the door with the jar tucked under his arm and the net propped on his shoulder.

Mom begins to clear away the dishes. "Bring him by on Monday. Gabby can show him around."

"But mom, I start school on Monday."

"You'll be home in the afternoon. No problem, right?"

"I guess not."

Rick slaps his cap back on his head and rises to leave. "I appreciate this, Bev. If he ever gets to be any trouble, you just send him back on over to my side of the fence. But like I said, he's a good kid. Nice seeing you again, Gabby."

Mom and dad see him off as he climbs behind the wheel of his truck and taps his horn. By the time he reaches the road, the rain is coming down in sheets, soaking everything in its path. Mom, dad, and I are assembled on the porch, watching the storm while Ryan plays in his treehouse. Any second now, someone is going to jump out from behind a bush and declare this was all an elaborate prank, including the part where my boyfriend leaves me to serve his country. But as the minutes tick by and no one comes, my stomach hollows with dread. Jayden is still gone, and now I have to play host-slash-tour-guide to our misogynistic neighbour's out-of-town nephew. If this whole situation doesn't prove men are the root of my problems…

"Well," dad says, "that's one less thing on my mind."

"When were you going to tell me you planned on hiring help?" I ask.

"I was getting around to it."

"This will be good for all of us," mom says. "Gabby will be able to focus on school, I'll be able to focus on Ryan, and you'll finally have an extra set of hands."

"I have hands," I say pathetically. I raise my arms in demonstration. "Or is it the rest of my female body that's the problem here?"

"This has nothing to do with you being female," dad insists. "It's about the fact that I want my daughter to go to college, get a proper education, and have a good life."

I mutter, "I thought *this* was the good life" and wave my arm at the dreary grey yard. "Fresh air, mud, the smell of cow poop wafting through my bedroom window twenty-four hours a day. What more could a girl ask for?"

"Working on a farm is proper, honest work, but I want more for you," dad tells me, wrapping his arm around my shoulder and kissing the crown of my head. "Besides, I thought you could use a friend right now."

Like I said, dad is the king of bad jokes. As he and mom head to the barn, I refill my Coke and retreat to the attic to think about Jayden and listen to Pink Floyd. All through the afternoon and into the evening, the storm batters the roof, proving that when it rains, it pours.

Chapter 2

"I can't believe you're doing this. Do you have any idea what I'm going through right now?" I say.

Mom is standing at the sink, peeling carrots for tonight's dinner. Ever since Rick's visit, I've launched an aggressive campaign to try and change my parents' mind about hiring help, especially if it's going to cost me my privacy.

She replies, "We're all going through something right now, Gabby—and that *something* is struggling to keep up with the farm." Her eyes flicker over me. "Unless you want to drop out of school and become a full-time farmer, we're going to need some help."

"But why do I have to share my room? Why not Ryan? God only knows he could use some positive male influence—"

"Ryan's room is a mess."

"Then make him clean it."

The vegetable peeler clangs against the side of the bowl. Mom doesn't get upset very often, but I can tell the stress is taking a toll on her by the way everything around us is slowly falling apart. So, she should understand exactly what I'm going through and tell Rick thanks, but no thanks, for the "help."

"The attic is big enough for two people," mom intones as she goes back to scraping the little white hairs off the carrots, "dad is going to build a wall to give you both some privacy. Think of it as being in college—everything there is co-ed."

"Not everything."

"I'm done discussing this. Now, please set the table."

I approach one of the cupboards and take down four plates from the shelf. My plan has always been to get as far away from this cow town as possible. Luckily, the changerooms at the fitness complex are not co-ed, or I'd be forced to give up the one thing I love even more than Jayden: swimming.

"Besides," mom says suddenly, dumping the orange ribbons into the trash, "it might be nice for you to have someone to talk to."

"Do you want me to talk to the help, or do you want me to act like there's a wall in my room and pretend he's not there?"

"I want you to treat him like a guest." She turns away from the counter at the same time that I go in search of cutlery. "Do you remember the first time I took you to the public pool?"

"Considering I was three years old, not really."

"You were so afraid to get in the water, I had to *beg* you to put on your water wings. You would've thought you were drowning with how much of a fuss you were making." She shakes her head and smiles. "But you got in the water. And look how far you've come."

"Oh, my god, mom. Get to the point before I develop PTSD."

"My point is, you have to give things a chance. Because right now, we need all the help we can get."

I bite my lip. When I was little, I got exceptionally good at holding my breath because I believed it was the only way to prevent myself from drowning. It was a passive form of protest, something that initially went unnoticed by my mother and the lifeguards at the pool. In the meantime, I learned how to paddle my arms and kick my feet until, slowly but surely, I lost my fear of drowning. But the habits you form when you're young and afraid tend to stick with you forever.

I let out a breath and set the knives and forks on the table. "Fine. Whatever makes you happy."

There's a wall in the middle of my room.

Dad built it yesterday, using a few studs and a couple sheets of plywood. It's the ugliest partition I've ever seen and makes my room smell like a lumber yard. As far as I'm concerned, it's enough of an injustice that I have to sleep in the attic while my brother gets his own bedroom on the second floor. But that's the way it's always been: Ryan's needs before my own.

This latest addition serves one purpose: to keep Vince and me, male and female, apart. "It's a small house," mom said as soon as dad started hauling in the building supplies. "Where else do you expect us to put our tenant?"

"Can't he sleep in the storage room in the barn? There's a space heater in there. He can watch over the cows at night."

"Oh, Gabby. Be reasonable. We want him to be well-rested if he's going to be productive."

"Well rested? Mom, I can barely breathe in my room. And it's not just because of all the dust. Can't you see I'm claustrophobic?"

Mom frowned at me and what she was quick to call "my selfish qualms." I asked her if she's ever felt overwhelmed and underappreciated, and she smirked and told me to wait until I have babies.

As for the wall, I'm not sure what to make of it. Dad had to maneuver the dresser from my roommate's side onto mine; it's tucked under the slope of the ceiling right now, while my desk is squeezed in between the plywood abomination and the bed. Worst of all, the already tiny window is now half the size, casting only a sliver of afternoon light on the floor.

I'm poring over an assignment for one of my classes when dad pokes his head into the attic. For the past hour or so, I've been glancing nervously at the clock, counting down the minutes until I look into the eyes of our new hired hand. At ten after four, the purring of an engine interrupts the usual sounds of the barnyard.

"They're here," he says.

"I know."

"Aren't you going to come meet your new neighbour?"

"I'm busy."

"Gabby." I look up at him. "Don't be rude."

I roll my eyes and push the chair away from the desk, then follow dad outside.

Rick offers his hand when we arrive. If I didn't know better, I'd think he's relieved to pass his nephew off to us.

"Good to see you again, Gus," Rick says. "I appreciate you opening your doors to Vince. You'll never have to worry about him making trouble."

I approach the congregation of adults—including mom, who has momentarily deserted her gardening duties to meet the hired help—with wary steps. At this point in the conversation, Vince slides out of the truck and ambles over to introduce himself.

"No, sir," he pipes up, "I prefer to keep to myself when given the choice. You won't even know I'm here."

Dad chuckles. "It's okay, Vince, we don't bite. Have you met Gabby?"

Vince reaches for my hand and gives it a perfunctory shake. "Now I have."

I force a smile and look at my shoes.

Mom chimes in, "You two will have plenty of time to get to know each other over the next little while. Gabby's really excited to have a roommate." I suppress the urge to sneer at mom's remark. Instead, I dig my toe into the dirt and flick a small stone off to the side.

"You're sure it's okay if I stay here?" Vince asks, apparently sensing my hesitation.

"Why wouldn't it be? There's plenty of room for one more," mom replies.

"Okay… Thank you."

Mom and dad smile at Rick, who peers at his watch and announces, "Well, I better be going. Take care, Vincent." He smacks his nephew on the shoulder and lumbers over to the driver's door of the truck. It rocks as he clambers in and pulls away from the house.

Mom, dad, Vince, and I stand in awkward silence as the dust settles around us. Ryan is milling about in his treehouse a few yards to my left. A Superman toy dips in and out of sight through the dirty window as Vince addresses me.

"I don't have to stay in the attic if you don't want," he says. "I have something of a gift for falling asleep anywhere. We can work out some other arrangement."

"Oh, don't be ridiculous, you're more than welcome." Dad slips an arm behind Vince's shoulders and leads him toward the house. "Speaking of which, why doesn't Gabby show you around a bit later? Can we get you anything in the meantime?"

"If it's not too much trouble. I mean, if you have something you need to—"

"Whatever. It's fine." I look at the ground, but my voice can't hide my disdain.

Vince turns back to mom. "Could I get a glass of water, please?"

He and my parents steer off in the direction of the kitchen, leaving me standing by myself outside the barn, wondering what the hell I've gotten myself into.

*

By the time my parents have finished fussing over Vince, I've fixed the barn for the night. I'm busy dumping grain into giant wooden storage containers when Vince appears behind me.

"Can I help you with that?" he offers.

I'm so startled by his voice that the bag of feed slips out of my hands and crashes to the floor; a mess of corn spills across the dirt, billowing into a cloud of dust.

Vince begins scooping the feed into the bag with his hands. "Sorry, Gabby, I thought you heard me come in."

"Whatever."

"It won't happen again."

"Look, it doesn't matter, okay?" I grit my teeth and go in search of a broom. I find one leaning against the wall of the storage room.

Vince is still trying to collect the kernels that have escaped behind the bins. He holds the bag open for me while I sweep the rest of the mess inside.

He smiles bashfully. "We make a pretty good team, don't you think?"

I roll my eyes. "Whatever."

"Is that the only response you know?"

I narrow my eyes. Vince stands the bag up and offers to pour the rest.

"Doesn't matter. Do what you want." I chuck the broom aside and walk toward the door. I'm nearly outside when his fingers close around my arm.

"Gabby?"

"What?"

"Are you okay? This isn't about the corn, is it?"

"I've already forgotten about it."

"I'm afraid you haven't."

"Vince, look, would you just forget about it? That sort of crap happens all the time."

"Why are you acting like a child? I'm just trying to help, Gabrielle."

"Don't," I say, "*ever* call me that again. It's Gabby. *Just* Gabby. Got it?"

Vince raises his hands.

"*Whatever*," he says. He brushes past me and tromps through the darkness back to the house.

Dinner ended twenty minutes ago. Since then, Vince has excused himself to unpack and dad's off helping Ryan with homework, which leaves mom and me to do the dishes. I'm staring out the window overlooking the tractor shed when mom plunges into a lecture about common courtesy.

"I can't believe you, Gabby. Ever since Jayden left you've been hiding in your room and mouthing off to the neighbors. Frankly, I'm ashamed." She scrapes the leftover mashed potatoes into a Tupperware container as I reach for another dirty dish. "I know you miss him, but it doesn't give you the right to turn your nose up at everyone else."

I'm at a loss for words, so I continue scouring the plate in my hand.

"And Vince. For Heaven's sake, he just got here. Couldn't you at least try to be polite?"

"What does it matter? I'll be at school most of the time. It's not like he cares how I act."

"He does care. Can't you see he's trying to connect with you?" Mom stares at me, willing our eyes to meet. As I indulge her with a hardened glance, she says, "Give him a chance. You might find you like him."

From the other room, Ryan's voice teeters on the verge of a total homework-induced meltdown. Something falls to the floor, and soon I hear dad's voice adding to the cacophony.

Mom sighs tiredly. "Sooner or later," she says as she strides out of the room, "something's gotta give."

While my parents attend to my hysterical brother, I disappear to the attic, where I find Vince lying on his bed, a book of some sort propped against his thighs. He looks entirely too comfortable for someone who's only been here for five hours. I lean against the wall and wait for him to look up from whatever he's doing.

Vince meets my gaze. "Is Ryan okay?" he asks.

I shrug. "Sure, just the usual homework mayhem. He'll get over it." I cross to my half of the room and plop down at my desk, where my grimy old history textbook mocks me with its uselessness.

Vince's voice fills the stuffy space. "Are you still upset about what happened in the barn?"

"I'm over it."

"Cool. So am I."

The only sound for a few agonizing seconds is the scratching of his pencil. I tilt my head to try and see what he's doing, but the wall blocks my view.

"You know, I could probably help him," Vince says suddenly.

"Who?"

The pencil's scraping stops momentarily. "Ryan. If it's math that's troubling him, I've got a few tricks up my sleeve."

I rise and go to the opposite half of the attic again. "Are you good at math?"

"Top of my class." Vince glances up. For some reason, I flinch.

"It's kind of funny, actually," he continues, "I've done nothing but move around my whole life. Since I couldn't hold on to any friendships I made, I vowed to keep up my grades instead. It's the one thing I've always had total control over."

"You like school," I say flatly.

"You could say that."

"Why?"

"Well, for one thing, it sure helps get through those tedious papers. And winter evenings would be loathsome without something productive to do."

"*Loathsome*? What are you, a hundred years old?" I stare at the book in his lap. "And what are you doing?"

Vince puts the finishing touches on his project and holds it up for me. An elaborate sketch of the water pump next to the house stares back from the creamy pages.

"You drew that?" I ask. "How long did it take you?"

Vince closes the book and replies, "A couple of hours. It was the first thing I saw when we pulled up."

"Oh."

"I could teach you some tricks, if you're ever interested in learning. But based on what I've seen so far, I think I'd be wasting my time."

I straighten up. "What's that supposed to mean?"

Vince thinks for a moment. "*Whatever. I don't care.*" He quirks a brow at me. "Sound familiar?"

"I'm tempted to call you an ass—or whatever fancy word you'd use to describe that part of the body."

"Well, the French say *le derrière.* But I don't suppose you know much French, given that your English vocabulary is so clearly lacking."

"Look, I'm being nice, letting you share my room. If you think I like this wall, you've got a problem."

"The only reason you're tolerating me is because you want something. Trust me, I grew up with six siblings. As soon as dad threatened to cut something off, they all turned into little angels."

"How old are you?"

"Old enough to recognize a child when I see one."

"Oh, look—another funny guy."

"Eighteen."

"I'm sixteen," I say haughtily, as if it makes any difference to our already vitriolic rapport.

"Well, I guess we know who runs the roost then, huh?" Vince smirks again and rises from the bed. "Now if you'll excuse me, it's been a long day. Don't mind if I hit the hay, do you?"

I scoff. "Fine by me."

Vince regards me with his intense green eyes for a minute. He mutters something under his breath as he descends the ladder and leaves the dimness of the attic for the welcoming chatter of the main floor.

*

I can't sleep. Vince keeps changing position, making the crummy old futon creak incessantly, and not even the hideous hunk of lumber can silence his restlessness. I close my eyes, but all it does is make me think of Jayden. Jayden, who used to fall asleep on our couch all the time without making a peep. Jayden, who's sleeping with a bunch of people he doesn't know. I wonder if he's made any friends. If he's thinking about me.

I bury my head in my pillow. Has the house always been this noisy? Normally, I'm so exhausted from working on the farm that I sink into a dead sleep without any difficulty. But this time is different, and it's all Vince's fault.

I roll onto my side and face the wall, startled by its formidable presence. I want the wall gone. I want Vince gone. And I want Jayden back. A rush of emotion clogs my chest, squeezing tears from my eyes. I draw a breath and hold it, wondering if Vince can hear me as well as I can hear him. But he doesn't say a word.

Figuring sleep is impossible, I roll out of bed and creep across the floor to the stairs. Once downstairs, I check over my shoulder to ensure no one has followed before slipping into my boots and out into the night.

To my left sits the driveshed, a three-sided structure comprised of wooden walls and a corrugated metal roof, where we keep our tractor and spare truck, plus other junk like water troughs and firewood. To my right, mom's rocking chair sways back and forth, inviting me to sit and stay awhile.

I ease myself into the chair and allow the gentle, rolling motions to lull me into a state of calmness. I imagine it's a week ago and Jayden is still with me, asking if he can smoke out here even though he knows the answer is no. *I don't know—can you?* is what I would say, and he'd just dazzle me with that romance novel smile and light up anyway. With Jayden, the answer is always 'yes.'

I drift off to sleep with the memory of his laugh reverberating in my ears.

Chapter 3

When Vince finds me the next day, I have a mean crick in my neck and my extremities are freezing. I gaze around as he hovers over me with his hands in his pockets.

"Don't you have school today?" he asks.

I run my fingers through my hair as I become aware of my surroundings. "What time is it?"

His eyes flick to his wristwatch. "7:23."

I stumble into the house and shower at record-breaking speed. A few minutes later, I zip through the kitchen and grab the slice of toast off Ryan's plate, then bolt out the door and down the driveway just as the bus is rolling away.

My best friend, Trisha, is waiting for me at the back. She's wedged between her own seat and the one in front, munching on a Triscuit and smiling at my disheveled state. I reach over and help myself to one of the crackers as I slide in beside her.

She nods at our driver and says, "You know, one of these days he's not going to stop."

"I wasn't that late. I was just running a little behind schedule."

The bus speeds toward the next stop. The girl in the seat next to us is huddled over a spiral-bound sketchbook. I casually crane for a glimpse of her creation, but she catches me peeking and shelters the book from view.

"So, who's the guy?" Trisha asks as she digs another cracker out of the bag.

"Who?"

"The guy who was standing on your porch. He waved, but I don't think you noticed."

"You mean Vince."

"I guess?"

"No one. Just the hired help."

Trisha prods me in the ribs. "*Just* the hired help?"

"Yes. He's only been here a day and I'm already sick of him." I wriggle deeper into the seat and let out a breath. "We share the attic."

"You share a room? Gabby, that sounds like the start of *something*, doesn't it?"

I nearly gag at the thought.

"You don't think?" I hear her say.

"Uh, no. Vince isn't my type. And just to jog your memory, I have a boyfriend."

"Oh, right. Jayden."

"And anyway," I say, "it's risky, getting involved with the hired hand. You don't want to have anything to do with someone who might disappear at any minute."

Trisha balls up her garbage and stuffs it into her bag, tearing the zipper shut. "True, but you could try to make the most of it."

"You don't know Vince. *I* don't know Vince, for that matter. His uncle dumped him at our place and took off like it was the most normal thing in the world. Vince doesn't have any friends, and he probably misses his family like crazy."

"Maybe those are good enough reasons to stay."

"What?"

"Gabby, think about it. I mean, if *I* had nowhere else to go, your place would seem like a good deal: fresh air, company, not to mention your mom bakes the best scones in the world. You should give him a chance."

I grumble, "You're beginning to sound like my mother."

"I'm only trying to help." She pulls herself up as the bus maneuvers into the school parking lot. "He's kind of cute, though, you have to admit."

"He's got *nothing* on Jayden."

Before long, we're swept away in the current of bodies traversing the halls. We split once we reach the stairs, and I head to my locker as she vanishes up to the second floor. As I walk, I replay our conversation in my mind, trying to wrap my head around what Trisha said. *Maybe those are good enough reasons to stay.* Maybe. Or, perhaps, they're even better reasons to leave. At eighteen, Vince has the legal privileges to pursue life on his own terms: he could leave at any time, and no one could stop him. Sooner or later, he'll lose interest in us, and my life will return to normal.

For some reason, though, in spite of what I said on the bus, I'm already doubtful.

It's raining again. As I make my way up to the house, I see the cows have sought shelter in the run-in dad constructed for them a few years ago. Their black-and-white coats are wet and matted, and specks of mud dot their legs. The occasional Holstein shakes her head, making her ears flap clownishly against her neck.

Ryan is seated at the kitchen table. Vince sits in the neighbouring chair, holding a pencil over a formula in Ryan's math book. When Vince sees me, he gives a nod of acknowledgement and resumes instruction. I wonder if he's still bristled by my brusque attitude from last night, or if it's already ancient history.

I drop my bag and raincoat in a heap on the kitchen floor, kick off my boots, and pour myself a cup of coffee. The tension in the air is palpable as I rummage around in the fridge for the milk carton. As I watch it swirl through the coffee, transforming the black brew like potions in a cauldron, I feel a sudden presence beside me.

It's Vince. Obviously.

"Do you take sugar in that?" he asks.

I glance at him. "Just a pinch."

He pops open the cupboard and takes down the sugar bowl. He finds me a spoon and places both within reach. Even though it's not his house, I'm flattered by his hospitality, and even more offended by my own bitterness.

"Thanks."

Vince shrugs. "It's the least I could do." There's a lull in our conversation as I sprinkle a small helping of the crystalline powder into my beverage and stir it slowly. "How was school?"

"Boring as hell. I can never get into it."

"It's only the second day. Things will pick up."

"That's what I'm afraid of."

Vince picks up the spoon and fiddles with it as I put the mug to my lips. He stares at his distorted reflection in the utensil before speaking again.

"You know, if you're ever having trouble with the content, I'm always available to help. At least in the short term."

"What does that mean?"

"This is only my second day here. I have yet to earn your parents' respect. I thought I would try and prove my competencies by giving Ryan some pointers, especially since you insinuated that math isn't his strong suit." Vince gestures to my brother with the spoon and mutters, "He's been cooperative so far."

"Well, it's a start."

"True. Rome wasn't built in a day."

The tension, which conversation briefly suspended, returns. I know something important is supposed to follow this sort of superficial interaction, but I'm at a loss for words right now.

Thankfully, Ryan speaks for me.

"You guys are weird," he says without turning around.

Vince laughs. "He's right." His eyes settle on me, and I notice their roundness for the first time.

I surprise myself by saying, "Could I talk to you… alone?"

Vince nods and extends his arm toward the living room. As we walk, I notice my pace hastening. When we stop, we end up on opposite sides of the coffee table.

I knead my fingers together. Across from me, his back to the huge stone fireplace, Vince waits patiently. Something in the way he stands reminds me of a bronze statue: the majority of his weight pinned on one leg, while the rest of his body hangs slack and supple.

Vince blinks. "Gabby?"

I shake my head. "Sorry, I was thinking about… David."

He raises a brow. "Who's David?"

"He's some statue we learned about in art class. By some guy named Donatello."

"Ah." He says this as though we've been carrying on a dynamic conversation about cats or gardening. Then, "Surely, that's not why you pulled me aside."

"No."

"So?"

I twirl a lock of hair around my finger. "I was a bitch to you last night. You deserve an apology."

Vince leans his heel on the edge of the hearth and says, "Apology accepted. Although, I think saying you were the b-word is an understatement."

"What would you have called me?"

"Stubborn. Antagonistic. Vile. Not that I can blame you, given the circumstances, but you could at least try to act your age."

"I *do* try."

"Doesn't look like it from where I'm standing."

"Yeah, well, you're an overachiever."

Vince smiles. "You could be, too. It's got nothing to do with upbringing or affluence. It's all about effort, Gabby."

"Some people are born talented. I'm not one of them."

"Talent is only a small part of success. The rest is all in here." He taps his chest, right in the spot where his heart is. "Saying that intelligence requires aptitude is like saying you need to be ripped *before* becoming a body builder. You understand?"

I shake my head.

"Simply put," Vince says, shifting to his other leg, "you don't have to go into anything already knowing how to do it. That's the fundamental principle of learning. If you knew how to do everything, life would stop being fun. Right?"

"You and I have a very different understanding of fun," I mumble.

He shrugs. "There are worse things than being boring." He checks his watch again. "Speaking of which, I'd better get back to helping Ryan. Then I've got some more work to do in the shed."

"You're always working, Vince," I say, following him.

He steers around the bulky leather armchair on his way back to the kitchen. "Not always. I eat and sleep like every other person I know. But I'm presuming you meant that in a hyperbolic sense."

"Are you always this technical… when you're not eating and sleeping like everyone else you know?"

He smirks, taking a seat next to my brother, who has lost focus and is now doodling in the corner of his notebook.

Vince lifts the textbook onto his lap and fans through the pages. "I try to articulate to the best of my abilities, to avoid any misinterpretations. But no, I'm not always like this." Our eyes meet and I'm struck by how bright his are, even in the dim grey of the storm-shadowed kitchen. His rectangular glasses capture the reflection of the window behind me.

Vince buries his face in the textbook as I slink away to the attic, where I remain until dinnertime.

✳

Two hours later, I'm drawn from my room by the delectable fragrance of a homecooked meal. I arrive downstairs to find Ryan planted in front of the TV, mesmerized by another episode of *Scooby Doo*, while Vince banters with my parents. He and dad are setting the table as mom rushes to pour tomato sauce on the spaghetti, toss the salad, and search fruitlessly for the breadbasket.

"I knew I had it here somewhere," she huffs as dad places the salad bowl on the table. "Gus, where—"

"Right here," Vince chimes in, reaching for the tongs on his way to the oven. He opens the door and removes each roll from the tray, laying them delicately in the cloth-lined basket. He smiles when he sees me in the doorway. "Gabby, you're just in time."

"*Just* in time," mom says. "Call your brother, will you?"

I do, then take a seat at the table. As expected, Vince assumes the spot right next to me.

Mom scurries around the kitchen. "All set? Good. Ryan!" She takes her place at the head of the table as my brother drags his feet into the room and climbs into the chair next to dad.

"I'm not hungry," Ryan moans.

"It'll come. Start eating." Dad drops a serving of spaghetti on his plate, then hands the dish across the table to Vince.

"Thank you, Mr. O'Connor."

Dad elbows my brother. "You see that, son?" he says. "You could learn a thing or two about etiquette from the young man."

Vince scoops some pasta for himself. "In my house, etiquette was the only thing that kept the order." He hands me the bowl; his fingers brush against mine as I accept it.

"So, Vince," mom says. I reach for a bun and rip it apart, etiquette be damned. "Surely, you must miss your family, having been displaced to the countryside all by yourself."

"It was my choice to leave home. I suppose you could say I was looking for room to grow, some place where I could drink life in."

Mom nods. "We were looking for the same thing, which is how we ended up out here. We wanted the kids to have a childhood they could look back on and be proud of. Besides, Gabby's made a lot of friends at school, haven't you, hon?"

I raise my brows and pick up a few lingering crumbs from around my plate. I can feel Vince watching me, though I'm not sure whether he's particularly impressed by my sizzling social life, given the total absence of his.

"Could you pass the salad?" I ask, looking anywhere but at him. Vince lifts the wooden bowl and holds it within my reach. He waits for me to say "Thank you" before going back to his meal.

Ryan pipes up, after driving the food around his plate without actually taking a bite. "But don't you miss your family?"

"Of course I do," Vince replies, although he doesn't look at Ryan as he speaks, "but it was time to move out. Nine people in one house gets a bit crowded."

"*Nine?*" Ryan gawks.

"Five daughters, two sons, and two parents. I'm the oldest child."

Ryan shifts his attention to me. "Their house must be huge!"

"Ryan, don't be rude," dad says, trying to suppress a smile that tells me he's thinking the same. "It's not nice to assume things about people."

"No, he's right—the house was a comfortable size," Vince interjects. "But sometimes feeling crowded isn't about space. It's about..." He flicks his gaze at me, and I make the mistake of looking like I care. "How much you want to grow."

"Have you ever lived in an attic before?" Ryan asks.

"No. Have you?"

"No. Gabby doesn't like to share her space."

"Really? I've actually felt quite welcome." If this is an attempt at sarcasm, then it's superb. If he's offering me an olive branch, I have no choice but to take it. After all, he's got the rest of my family wrapped around his finger.

"I'm glad you're enjoying your stay," I say in a controlled voice.

"So, what's next, Vince?" dad asks. "College? Work?"

Vince swallows. "I'm planning to go to university, then teacher's college if I can afford it. I haven't gotten around to applications yet, but I intend to do so in the near future."

"You and Gabby should work together then," mom says. "It's still a bit early for her to be thinking about post-secondary, but it would be good for a first taste."

"Certainly," Vince enthuses, "that would be great. I could use the input, to be honest."

A few minutes later, he rises from the table, collects his empty plate, and carries it to the sink. "Thank you for dinner, Mrs. O'Connor. I'm sorry to have to run off but I still have some work to do, so if you'll excuse me…"

Across the table, Ryan slides out of the chair and bolts from the room to return to his previous television euphoria. Vince is in the middle of packaging the leftovers when dad says, "You've worked enough for one day, Vince. Why don't you let Gabby finish up in the barn? Can I get you a coffee, or are you more of a tea kind of guy?"

Vince's eyes dart quickly between us. I save him the dilemma by collecting my jacket and boots and vanishing outside, where I'm confronted by an unpleasant chill. I stand for a minute on the porch, letting the icy dampness of the air cut through the flush in my cheeks. Soon, I hear the door open behind me.

"I feel bad about this," Vince admits. "Let me give you a hand with the cows. It'll only take a few minutes between the two of us."

"Don't bother. I managed fine without you before. Might as well get back to your coffee… or tea." Pulling my hood over my ears, I trot down the steps. I follow the fence that parallels the driveway, dodging puddles as I go and stewing over my unfortunate situation. My boot kicks a stone, which bounces a few feet away and rolls into the grass. For the hell of it, I clobber a few more rocks until I finally reach the barn.

Something prompts me to look back at the house. Sure enough, I see Vince swaying in the rocking chair: waiting, always waiting, for me to bounce back.

Chapter 4

"I don't know," I say, picking at the crust of my sandwich. "Vince seems so…"

"Perfect?" Trisha proffers. She sucks on the straw sticking out of a bottle of Sprite. "No one's perfect, Gabby."

"I know, but this guy is as close as you can get. He *never* stutters. And his gaze is so intense he could probably liquefy your brain. He even helps to make dinner!"

"Aw. That's so cute."

"Maybe. It would be cuter if he wasn't trying so hard to impress my parents."

"Your parents," Trisha says pointedly, "or you?"

"Please, he's smart enough to know I'm not interested in him. Besides, I've already got a boyfriend."

"Vince doesn't know that."

"He should."

"Look." Trisha puts down her drink. "I know you're mad about Jayden leaving, but try not to take it out on the new guy. Your parents obviously need him around. And who knows? Maybe you and Vince will even become friends."

"Don't hold your breath."

Trisha digs her phone out of her backpack and grimaces. "I have to take this." She slides back her chair and slips from the room to answer the call.

After she leaves, I take my own phone out of my bag and study the training schedule my swimming instructor, Tanya, sent me. For me, swimming is more than a hobby—it's my escape from the stress of everyday life, a way to feel powerful when I'm utterly powerless. Tanya has been ratcheting up the pressure lately, adding more laps and tougher strokes to my regimen in hopes I'll cave and sign up for the Spring Swim-a-thon. With Vince breathing down my neck, I may not have a choice.

A few minutes later, Trisha returns looking thoroughly put out. "Sorry about that. Sisters always find a way of being annoying."

"So do hired hands," I say.

"Are you sure you're not putting that flaw on him yourself? Maybe it's all in your head."

"Now, why would I do that?"

"Because… you feel crowded. Or threatened. At least, that's how it sounds, from everything you've told me."

"By Vince? He doesn't scare me. He's scrawny and easy to overpower. Jayden could lift him by his shirt with one hand."

"I don't mean in a physical way."

"The point is, this isn't going to work. He has *got* to go."

"Go *where*? The streets? He's not a hobo, for crying out loud!"

"He's not a farmer either! Whose side are you on, Trish?"

"No one's."

I gather my belongings, heap the waste on the plastic tray, and stand up.

"Gabby, come on, don't you think you're being just a *little* sensitive?"

"About what? I don't want to talk about Vince now. It's making me hate him more."

"You have no reason to hate him. He's just a guy."

"He's not, though. If you met him, you'd know what I mean."

Trisha stands up as well. She tosses her empty Sprite bottle into the recycling bin, slings her bag over her shoulder, and falls into step beside me as we head back to my locker. "You know what the real problem is here?"

"No."

"You're used to having your way."

"I am not."

"No? Remember last year, when we had to do that presentation on world cultures? We were supposed to work on it together, but the night before it was due, you went out with Jayden and I finished the whole thing myself."

"I remember that. We got an A."

"*I* got an A. You got a hickey. There's no such thing as a team effort when it comes to you."

I want to scream with how untrue this is. No such thing as a team effort? Teams are supposed to work together, not clamber for the top spot on the pyramid and crush the people down below. "I know all about being a team player."

"Oh, do you? Then prove it. Work out your differences with Vince." Trisha shakes her head. "I have to get to class."

Before I even manage to come up with a half-decent reply, Trisha steps around me and walks away. I watch her until she disappears from view and I can no longer hear the clack of her boots on the tile floor.

*

I return home feeling unusually spent. The house is empty when I arrive, and darkness is already seeping into the rooms. I peer at the note on the kitchen table:

Gabby— We've taken Ryan to buy some new skates. Your dad and I have some business at the bank and won't be home until later. Please go ahead and heat up the soup we left in the fridge.

Mom

PS. Vince has offered to drive you to swimming.

I tear off the note and scrunch it into a ball. Taking the soup out of the fridge, I spoon it into a bowl and stick it in the microwave to heat. As the food spins around inside its tiny oven, the front door opens and Vince walks in.

He looks flustered. "Hi."

"What?"

"You look frustrated."

I unknot my brows, feeling the creases on my forehead smooth away. "It's nothing."

I wait for him to pry, to say something that will go right over my head. Instead, he walks over to the sink and cranks on the water. I watch as the soapy lather cleanses the filth from his skin, then say, "Mom says you'll drive me to my lesson tonight."

He dries his hands on the towel. "I'm only trying to help."

"Sure."

We stand in silence, shouldering the weight of unspoken words. There's a smear in the shape of a handprint on Vince's shirt, and his hair is disheveled around his ears.

I point to his outfit. "Been playing in the mud?"

"Fixing the tractor, actually."

"You don't seem like the type. You're more of a bookworm… aren't you?"

Vince shrugs. "You pick up a lot of skills, moving around as much as I did."

"Interesting."

"I thought so. Anyway, you can tell your dad it seems to be working again, though if you ask me, I think it's on its last legs." Vince sniffs the air as the soup smell fills the kitchen. "What's cooking?"

"Leftover soup." I falter. "Do you want some?"

"I am a little famished."

"Just say 'hungry.' We're not in a black and white TV show." The microwave timer beeps, and I take out my scalding bowl of soup before setting it on the table. As I turn back to the counter, Vince picks up the spoon and holds it out to me, miming an obsequious server.

"Thank you," I grit.

"Bad day?"

Anger flashes behind my eyes. It fades rapidly when I think of what Trisha said at lunch about saddling Vince with nonexistent flaws as a way to distance myself from his kindness—the kindness I don't deserve because of how I've been acting since Jayden moved away.

I loosen my grip on the spoon and sigh. "You could say that."

"Do you want to talk about it? I promise I won't interrupt."

"That's okay. I'd rather just eat."

"Works for me."

As I sit down and start eating, I instantly feel better. Mom doesn't like it when I eat big meals before swim practice, but the warm soup is doing a marvelous job of melting whatever cold feelings I still have toward Vince. He moves around the kitchen without speaking, putting away this and that, until the microwave times out and he joins me at the table, bending over his bowl as if I'm not even present.

I stare down at the minestrone. "My best friend thinks I'm not a team player, but she's wrong. I'm good at working with other people."

Vince continues to stir his soup as he says, "If you say so."

"I am."

He lifts his gaze, a smile teasing the corners of his mouth. "A family is a team too, you know. Everyone has to pull their weight in order for it to succeed."

"You don't think I do that?"

"I think there's some room for improvement."

I scowl at his imperious tone. "You know what else a team is supposed to do? Support its weakest members."

"That's also true. But you're not weak, Gabby."

Well, that's not what I was expecting at all. I rest my spoon in my empty bowl, hating the sound it makes as it echoes around the room. Nothing kills a fight faster than kindness, and Vince is boiling over with niceness.

"You're not weak either," I say softly. "In fact, I think you're the pack leader. Like a wolf."

"Actually, I've read that wolf packs don't have a single leader. In the wild, a group of wolves is really just a family consisting of a monogamous mating pair, their pups, and occasionally some young adults who aren't ready to be independent yet. Kind of like humans."

I shake my head. "Of course you know so much about wolves." Darting a glance at my backpack, I ask, "What do you know about physics?"

"Kinematics, vectors, some practical applications."

"Do you want something to do for a while?"

"Sure, as long as it's not your homework."

I scrape back my chair and transfer my bowl to the sink. "Never mind, then."

"You'll never learn that way."

"Why are you so hung up on learning? Do you do anything other than study?"

"Like what?"

I flail my arms. "I don't know. Like... go shopping or... go on dates. *Something.*"

Vince clears his dishes from the table.

"For one," he says, "I don't buy what I don't need. I buy for friends and family on occasion, but my list of wants is extremely short. As for dates…"

"You've set the bar unreasonably high, and everyone falls short of your expectations?"

He frowns. "I was going to say I usually get turned down, but I suppose we all have expectations."

"*You* get turned down?"

"In case you haven't noticed, I know a lot about wolves and nothing about pop culture. You do the math." Vince refers to his watch. "We should head out. Just give me a few minutes to change into something decent."

"I need to get my stuff anyway."

Vince and I head for the living room at the same time and fall into an awkward tango to let the other pass. At the stairs, it's the same thing—a veneer of excessive politeness to hide our annoyance at the other's dawdling. Finally, Vince insists on letting me proceed, although I can't say I'm a fan of feeling his warm breath on the back of my neck.

Once we reach the attic, I say, "You first."

"Are you sure?"

"I'm sure. Seriously."

The stairs leading to the attic creak with each of Vince's steps. As soon as I pop my head through the opening, the dusty fragrance of wood and cardboard boxes bears down on me. Vince crouches next to the bed and slides his suitcase out to hunt for a change of clothes.

As I ferret through my dresser for my swimsuit and cap, he says, "Could you give me a moment?"

"Yeah, one sec." I can't find my swimsuit. I know mom washed it, but since I hate folding laundry, it undoubtedly got mixed in with my everyday clothes. One second turns into five, then ten, but no matter how much I dig, the spandex material eludes me.

I make the mistake of looking over my shoulder. The dresser may be on my half of the attic, but it's as far from the wall as Vince and I are from being friends—especially now that he has his shirt off.

I go back to looking for my goggles, trying to shake the image from my mind as I paw through my clothes.

He approaches from behind, now donning a pastel blue polo shirt with opaque white buttons. "Ready?"

I bag my gear and bump the drawer closed with my elbow. "Sure."

"You saw, didn't you? Even with a wall, a guy can't get any privacy around here."

"I didn't see… much."

Vince chuckles. "That's all right. When I was a kid, we lived in a small apartment with only one bathroom. Where I'm from, privacy is a luxury, not an expectation."

"So, you're not embarrassed?"

"So you *did* see."

"It was an accident, okay? The wall's not a perfect solution. Don't go thinking there's anything going on between us."

He raises his hands as we leave the attic. "Okay. But you know, I think we're making progress here."

"We're not. I turned around when I shouldn't have."

"Liar."

"Whatever."

Vince quickens his step to keep up with me. I zip up my windbreaker at the same time that Vince pockets the keys to dad's truck.

"I just find it strange," he continues. "You don't even try to defend your position. I expect teenage girls to be more… headstrong."

"I suck at arguing. You happy? I said it. Now your ego can be *that* much bigger, because you found one more thing that you're better at than me."

Vince shakes his head. "What are you *talking* about, Gabby?"

"Oh, quit playing dumb. Ever since you came here you've done nothing but try to be better than me at *everything*. Math, cooking, fixing things…"

He rakes a hand through his sandy hair. "Look, Gabby…" I open my mouth to protest, but he waves a finger at me. "Let me finish. Ever since I arrived you have been insolent and bitter. Not everything is a competition. Name one thing I've done to you besides trying to be friends. Besides trying to *help* you."

"I don't need your help, Vince. And I sure as hell don't need you trying to make me something I'm not."

"What? A better person?"

I scowl. Vince remains firm in his stance, studying me, waiting, always waiting…

"Let's go," I say at last.

Vince shrugs. "Okay."

He holds the door open for me as we leave.

*

Against my wishes, Vince follows me into the fitness complex and makes himself comfortable on one of the benches by the pool. The air reeks of chlorine and soggy towels as I emerge from the changeroom wearing my swimsuit. I start in on my stretches and hope no one will inquire about my visitor.

Tanya, my swimming coach of eight years and dad's would-have-been fiancée, sidles up to me. As always, she's wearing white shorts, a red t-shirt, and a whistle around her neck. Her tawny hair is combed back into a sharp ponytail, which somehow makes her face look as young as a cherub and as dignified as a queen.

"You made it," she says. "And about time, too."

I straighten up and stretch my arms behind my head. "I would've been here earlier, except I got hung up at home." I pass Vince a sidelong glance. When he turns his head toward us, I pretend we've never met.

He waves anyway.

Tanya reciprocates. "Who's your friend?" she asks me.

"Vincent McCarthy. He's not my friend."

"Oh. Then who is he?"

"Some guy dad hired to help. But he's not helping so much as completely taking over my job."

"Really? He doesn't look like the type." She smirks. "Besides, I think he likes you."

I'm about to remind her of Jayden when Tanya starts fudging with my swimming cap, saying, "So, are you here to talk about boys, or are you here to practice your strokes?"

"I don't want to talk about boys."

"That's what I thought."

Tanya motions to the pool. Ten feet deep and eight lanes wide, it's as big as the ones they use in the Olympics. In between each lane is a necklace of floats in an alternating red-and-white pattern—much prettier than the plywood partition I'm used to back home, though it serves virtually the same purpose. The water is breathtakingly clear with a pale blue tint from the tiles lining the walls. Looking at it, you can almost forget you're surrounded by farmland and unimaginative, cookie-cutter houses.

My warmup routine finished, I walk along the edge of the pool and step up onto one of the black starting blocks. I pull my goggles down over my eyes and adjust their fit. The floor ripples beneath the shimmering surface as I lean forward and grasp the front of the block with my fingers. I gather my composure, check to see if Vince is watching (his attention is riveted on me), and at the sound of Tanya's whistle, dive headfirst into the water.

I vanish into a stream of bubbles, using my entire body to propel myself forward. The water feels like a second skin, smooth and cool to the touch. After a few seconds underwater, I break the surface for a quick gulp of air, then go facedown again for maximum speed. My arms move in an alternating rhythm, pulling my body from side to side. Tanya stands at the finish line, hollering words of encouragement and criticism.

"Good head position, Gabby," she says. "But you're still bending your knees too much. It's like you're trying to slow yourself down on purpose."

I reach the end of the pool and lean on the rough surface. "I was just getting started."

"I hope so. Do a couple of backstrokes and hop back on the block." She walks away, off to check on another student.

Vince's shadow looms over me. He's grinning like a child who's been to Disneyland.

"Gabby, that was amazing. Where did you learn to dive like that?" He crouches and skims the water with his fingertips.

"Here. I've been perfecting my technique since I was about eight. Well, I've been swimming since I was three, but Tanya's a tough coach, so I advanced pretty quickly."

"That's incredible."

I try to be stoic, to appear as though his flattery has no effect on me, but I feel a blush creep into my cheeks anyway. "It's nothing."

Vince's eyes soften. "Still, it's impressive. Better than anything I could do even if I started today."

I smile and backstroke to the starting block. Over and over again, Tanya makes me practice my freestyle and breaststrokes, lectures me about drag, and gives me five more reasons why I should enter the competition. An hour and a half later, I'm back in the truck with Vince.

"I appreciate you letting me stay," he says after we've been driving for five minutes.

"Well, where else would you have gone? It's not like there's anything to do in this town."

"Is that why you took up swimming—to have something to do?"

"No. I took up swimming because I enjoy swimming." I look over at him. Vince smiles. "What?"

"You give straight answers. I like that about you." He says, "Would you mind if I asked you something else?"

"Shoot."

"Have you considered competing? With all due respect, it's a waste of time to sharpen your skills without challenging your comrades to outdo you."

"I don't have any comrades. Who even uses that word in casual conversation?"

"I do. And you would find some, if you escalated your training and registered for some competitions. Who knows where they might take you?" Vince turns to look at me. The silence hangs heavy in the air as we bump along the rocky road back to the farm.

"I used to," I finally say.

"Used to what?"

"Compete." I thread my fingers through my hair, wondering whether admitting defeat would pump Vince's ego even more. *To hell with it.*

"When I was a little kid, my mom signed me up for swim classes— mostly so I'd be safe around water. Over time, I fell in love with the sport. A few of my friends from school had swimming pools, and whenever they had birthday parties, I'd be outside practicing my flutter kicks while everyone else was inside eating cake."

"Swimming must've been pretty important to you, if you gave up cake for it," Vince says with a smirk.

"I gave up everything for it." I pause. "As time went on, mom and dad started letting me sign up for competitions. Nothing major or anything—just local meets with other kids. I was super competitive though, and eventually I became bored with swimming laps. So, I developed an obsession with diving."

"Diving?"

"Yes. Diving, as in off a springboard. And since I was already a confident swimmer, I didn't think twice about getting hurt."

My throat tightens and I look away, out the window at the trees streaking along the road. Vince is silent and still in the driver's seat. Waiting, as always.

"One day, I decided to try a more complicated dive that I'd only practiced a couple of times with Tanya: a reverse with a half-twist. But I didn't leave enough room between myself and the board, and as I went to do the twist, I hit my head. That's the last thing I remember from that day."

Vince's eyes jump from the driveway to my face and linger there. His mouth opens slightly, but for once, he has no speech prepared. He's stunned, like I was that day at the pool, sinking down to the bottom and unable to scream for help.

The silence makes me want to keep talking. "After that, I didn't want to swim anymore. Mom said I had to get back on the horse, and after a couple of months I got back in the water, started training again. But every time I saw that diving board my whole body would tense up. It took years for me to even think about competing again, and…"

"I'm sorry. I had no idea. I didn't mean to bring up painful memories."

"It's okay. You just got here." I look at him, but only for a second. The light above the barn shines brightly in the dark and reflects off the frame of his glasses. "So what's your diving board story?"

"I'm not sure I understand what you're asking."

"Everyone has a painful memory—a story about how they quit something they loved. And a guy like you has to have at least one chink in his armour."

"A guy like me." We roll up to the house and stop. "So you're admitting I'm a knight in shining armour."

I should've known my careless word choice would backfire. His supercilious smirk is merely a formality.

"Just answer the question," I snap.

"No. I don't have a diving board story."

Of course he doesn't. "Colour me shocked." I reach between my feet for my swim gear and open the door with my other hand. My shoes roll over the small stones as I walk up to the front door, with Vince casting a dull shadow in my periphery. I don't believe him: everyone has weak spots, and he wouldn't be trying so hard to appear perfect if he wasn't trying to conceal his own vulnerabilities.

Mom is sitting in the living room when we enter. The house is surprisingly quiet, which means Ryan is probably not doing homework, but playing up in his room. Vince closes the door behind us, then hangs up his jacket and neatly stashes his shoes by the door, checking off every box on the houseguest etiquette list.

I toss my stuff on the floor as mom asks, "How was swimming?"

"Fine. I worked on refining my technique for the millionth time." I flop down on the sofa, exhausted from the day's excruciations. Above the rumbling of the TV, I can hear Vince putting away the dishes, making himself useful.

Mom collects her mug from the coffee table and dunks her teabag a couple of times to release the last bit of flavour. "Any word on when the competition schedule will be posted?"

"No, but it doesn't matter. I'm not entering."

Mom frowns. As far as she's concerned, I have an obligation to flaunt my skills to a rapt audience, if only to justify keeping dad's ex in our lives. Considered from this angle, I can kind of see why it matters.

Still, swimming competitions are brutal. The training is intense, the risk of severe injury is high, and the pressure is debilitating. But with school, the farm, and ignoring Vince (which is a full-time job on its own), I'm fully booked.

In this moment, Vince enters the room and immediately scans the place for something to do. When his search turns up empty, he addresses mom. "How can I be of assistance, Mrs. O'Connor?"

Mom smiles. "By resting. You need your sleep, too."

As if on cue, Vince suppresses a yawn. It's satisfying, this tiny glimmer of humanity. It can almost make you like the guy if, like me, you're on the fence about trusting him.

"You know, I think I'll do that—as long as Gabby doesn't need anything."

I consider his offer. If I told him I wanted a hot chocolate or a slice of blueberry pie or the answers to life's biggest questions, he'd undoubtedly jump at the chance to prove how smooth and shiny his metaphorical armour really is. But one look at his face changes my mind.

"I'm good," I tell him. Vince nods imperceptibly before turning away, so clearly fatigued that he doesn't even bother to lecture me on the quality of my reply.

Mom waits until he's good and gone before putting a voice to her thoughts. "Well? Is he as awful as you imagined he'd be?"

"Worse," I mutter.

"It's nice to see you two getting along."

"You call this getting along? I can barely open my mouth without getting a lecture from him." My eyes flicker toward the stairs. "Did you and dad really need the help, or were you just doing Rick a favour?"

"We needed the help. Ryan's still too young to operate the equipment and you're busy with school and swimming. And Rick didn't dump Vince here like a stray cat—we approached him and asked if one of his sons was interested in earning some extra money."

"They all said no?"

"They're busy too. But Rick knew Vince was going to be in town, so he asked him if he'd be interested in gaining experience on a dairy farm."

"And he jumped at the opportunity," I conclude. It's tough to imagine Vince doing anything halfheartedly: either he plunges in with both feet, or he graciously lets someone else go ahead of him. Even in my mind, he finds ways to be insufferable.

Mom shrugs. "I don't know. All I know is we're happy to have him for as long as he's available."

"I'm sure you are." I swing my legs off the couch. "I'm going to bed."

"Love you," she says as I shuffle out of the room.

"Sure you do," I reply, smirking at her over my shoulder. I climb the stairs to the second floor, then walk to the bathroom to brush my teeth. Vince is coming out when I get there. He's wearing soft cotton pajama pants and a plain white t-shirt, and there's a towel draped over his right shoulder. When he sees me, he smiles and heads straight for the attic, but I can't get mom's words out of my head.

"Bathroom's all yours," he tells me.

"Thanks." I bite my lip. "Hey, Vince?"

"Yeah?"

"What made you want to come here? I know you need the money, but why our farm? You could've stayed with your uncle and gotten the same experience."

He considers his response carefully. "I don't think I really had a choice in the matter. My uncle didn't have much space and your father needed help."

"That's it?"

"That's it." His smile remains, even as his feet retreat. "Goodnight, Gabby."

So that's it—a story without a twist. Vince saw an opportunity and dove in without a second thought. I guess it's a good thing he can't swim, or I'd never stand a chance.

Chapter 5

The remainder of the week drags by. Dad keeps Vince busy with work around the farm, and I stick to my usual routine, which consists of going to school, listening to Trisha complain about her older sister, Caitlin, and waiting for Jayden to call. Whenever we pass each other in the hallway, Vince always smiles and asks how I am, even if the answer is crystal clear on my face. He's relentlessly friendly. Nauseatingly polite. I keep expecting his skin to turn green like an alien's, or for a screw to fall out of his ear, or to see some other incontrovertible proof that he's not human, because no one tries this hard to stay on the straight and narrow unless they've already veered wildly off-course.

Despite myself, I work up the nerve to approach him on Saturday morning, after hours of trying to wrap my mind around Shakespeare's twisted prose. I find Vince in the driveshed, changing the tires on the spare truck.

He turns the jack until the old Ford is a few inches off the ground. Clutching *Macbeth* to my chest, I slap a smile on my face and ask, "Still got all your fingers?"

He turns around and grins, holding up both hands for me to see. "So far, so good."

"I had no idea you were so handy."

He roots through the dusty toolbox at his feet, producing a socket wrench from the disarray. "That's what I get for being the man of the house."

It takes me a second to realize he's talking about his own house, the one he left in order to come and help us. All I know about Vince's family is that he moved often and has a lot of siblings. That's a lot of potential diving board stories.

I wade in slowly. "Did your dad teach you how to do all this?" I make an arbitrary gesture toward dad's truck. It has a lackluster orange body, an old-fashioned grill, and a ribbed silver steering wheel the size of a hula hoop. He's been holding on to the old clunker until I get my G2, but I'd rather walk than be seen in this death trap.

Vince finally answers, "My dad was a mechanic. Working on cars together was how we bonded, when he had time to spend with me. But he's long gone now."

"I'm sorry. When did he die?"

"Oh, he's not dead. My parents are divorced. My biological parents, I mean. Long story."

I thumb through the book. "Anyway, I know you're busy, but I was wondering if you knew anything about Shakespeare."

"I know he was born in Stratford-upon-Avon in 1564. He had a wife and three children. Oh, and he died on his birthday. Not many people know that, but it's true."

"You know a lot about Shakespeare," I observe, realizing this could be a double-edged sword for me. Either I'm living with a hard-core literature nerd who may be my only hope of salvaging my English grade, or Vince has found a new way to torment me.

"I know a lot about a lot of things." He loosens the bolts on the nearest tire.

"What do you know about *Macbeth*?"

"It's a revenge plot gone wrong. It's one of Shakespeare's bloodiest plays too, which is really saying something given that most of his work favoured violence and brutality."

Vince stands up and pulls the almost bald tire off its axel. He rolls it off to the side and picks a brand new one off the stack to his right. Sweat dampens his armpits and hairline. It's not the proof I've been looking for, but it's a start. Still, no normal eighteen-year-old should know this much about a guy who died hundreds of years ago.

"What did you ever do before I came along?" Vince asks suddenly.

My focus sharpens at his question. "What do you mean?"

"I don't mind helping Ryan with his homework, but you seem a bit old to need all the answers."

"I don't need all the answers."

"Then why are you out here?"

"I *live* here. And if I'm being honest, my life kind of sucks right now, so if you could decide whether or not you're going to help me, that would be great."

Vince tests the newly fitted tire and brushes his hands together. Then he picks up the iron and moves to the opposite side of the vehicle.

"The lady doth protest too much," he mutters. Soon, Vince crouches and disappears from view.

"What did you say?"

"It's a line from *Hamlet*, spoken by Gertrude, in regards to her reaction to a character in a play."

"I thought we were talking about *Macbeth*," I protest. At least he's made up his mind about helping me. "You seriously need to get a hobby—or a girlfriend."

Vince pops up from behind the truck. I can't tell if my comment has offended him, since he's made an effort to smile and even nod in agreement. He raises a hand to his brow and wipes away the sheen of moisture, leaving a streak of filth in its place.

"Yeah," he drawls, "or I could get back to work."

"You could do that." I'm about to turn away when Vince once again rubs his forehead. This time, a pale pink scar appears at the edge of his hairline.

"Did you hurt yourself?" I wonder aloud, pointing to the blemish.

Vince liberates the old tire from the axel and sets it off to the side. "A long time ago."

"What happened?"

"I hit my head on the corner of the kitchen table. My mother came running in and found me covered in blood. Dad took me to the hospital to get stitches. I was pretty young at the time, so I don't remember how many. Afterwards, he took me to get ice cream."

"How did you hit your head, exactly? Did you fall?"

"Yes."

"And you didn't try and catch yourself?"

"It all happened very quickly," he snaps. "Now I really do have to get back to work—and so do you." He indicates my dog-eared copy of *Macbeth*. He's not smiling this time, although he has the decency to look apologetic.

I turn and stalk back to the house. I should feel relieved—Vince isn't an alien, after all. He's human. And if someone like him can fail, then where does that leave me?

*

I never manage to make sense of *Macbeth*, nor do I have any further interaction with Vince. Now, as I help mom peel potatoes for dinner, our conversation has crept to mind again.

"I see Vince did some work on the spare truck," mom says as she tenderizes the chicken. "He's quite handy in the garage, don't you think?"

"Yeah." I reach for another potato and remove its papery skin with the peeler. "His dad taught him a bunch of stuff about cars, but then his parents got divorced." I ask, "Did you notice the scar Vince has on his forehead?"

"I didn't."

"He said he fell when he was a kid. He went into a lot of detail about it."

"Well, kids do the darnedest things. Just look at Ryan."

"Yeah, but it's *Vince*. He does everything perfectly, in case you haven't noticed."

"Hmm."

"So you agree with me?"

"About Vince being perfect? No. If you ask me, you have far more important things to worry about than what the hired hand is doing."

Mom shoots me a sidelong glance. My mediocre GPA isn't exactly a secret, but it has been the subject of numerous late-night conversations between my parents. The fact that I'm usually awake to hear them is undeniably part of the problem.

"How are your grades?" she asks, going back to her cooking.

"They're okay. I tried asking Vince for help, but he was busy."

"As he should be."

In that moment, Vince walks through the door. He's covered in dirt, grease, and sweat. He removes his glasses, which are also flecked with debris, and polishes the lenses with the hem of his shirt.

"Well, don't you look like you've been having fun out there," mom jokes as Vince bends to untie his shoes.

"Fun," he replies, "or maybe frustration." He takes off his shoes. "Would you mind if I took a quick shower, Mrs. O'Connor? I'm quite certain you wouldn't appreciate me attending dinner in this deplorable state."

"You don't have to ask, Vince," she tells him. "Go ahead. We'll wait for you."

Vince thanks her, gives me a little wave, and strides out of the kitchen to the upstairs bathroom.

I dump the peels into the garbage bin and pass the potatoes over to mom, who submerges them in boiling water. I tell her I'm going to do homework, which she acknowledges with a nod before turning her focus back to the dinner preparations.

In the attic, I pull out my books and channel my energy on some physics formulas. Outside, Ryan romps around the front yard while dad fusses with the cows. A few minutes pass before I hear him start up the tractor: a couple coughs, and soon it's running like a dream.

*

"Step right up!" a man in a red suit calls into the crowd. "You want a prize? We got prizes. All sizes of prizes! What about you, little man? You want a prize?"

Ryan breaks into an enormous grin, tempted by the sight of life-sized plush tigers and sparkly white unicorns with purple manes that dangle from the roof of the midway stand. He's so annoying and goofy that I can't help but smile, too.

The Red Suit Man—the fall fair version of Santa Claus—belts out a hearty laugh and tells my brother, "Well, don't just stand there, step right up! It's five dollars for three balls. Hit one target, get a small prize. Hit two targets, get a medium prize. Hit all three targets, win a giant prize!" He motions to the animals above his head.

Ryan turns to me expectantly. "Can I have five dollars?"

I almost say no; everyone knows these games are rigged, but the fair only comes to town once a year. Besides, he's guaranteed to lose interest once he sees the prizes are mainly for display.

I hand him a blue bill and watch his face light up like a sparkler.

"Alright, let's see what you got, little man." The man steps aside as Ryan swaggers up to the booth. Three wooden targets with faded white bull's eyes stare back at him. He reels back his arm, takes aim at the one on the left, and pitches the first ball with audible effort. The projectile arcs through the cool autumn air and whizzes straight past the target, banging against the wall with disappointing finality.

"Oh, so close!" I wonder how much the game host gets paid to feed these kids all this false hope. He says, "You still have two more targets. Hit them both, and this little fella is yours!" His fingers squeeze the medium-sized gorilla off to the side.

Ryan gets behind his next pitch. The second target wobbles as the ball skims its top.

"Better luck next time!" The man moves toward a small prize now, a little stuffed dog with blue spots and a pink, heart-shaped nose.

My brother concentrates. Squints his eyes. Scrunches his nose. His fingers close on the third and final ball, and it takes me a moment to realize I'm holding my breath. Yes, he's a pain in the ass most days, but he's my little brother and I want more than anything to see him succeed.

The target snaps backwards, a perfect bull's eye. Ryan squeals with delight and leaps into the air.

"Well done! Step right up and claim your prize!" The man unhooks the blue-spotted pup from the bunch and hands it to Ryan, who's beaming like someone just gave him a million bucks. I guess to a kid, they're basically the same thing.

We thank the guy and blend back into the crowd. The air is thick with the smell of funnel cake, deep-fried Oreos, caramel popcorn, and barnyard animals, lowing, bleating, and clucking away in the agricultural building behind the midway. A lady around mom's age is whipping up a fresh batch of cotton candy. Ryan's mouth is watering at the sight of those pastel clouds, and because I'm in a particularly good mood today, I slip him another five.

"Thanks, Gabby," he says, eyeing the money. "Why are you being so nice to me?"

"You're my kid brother. And it's the fall fair. Don't get used to it, though." I give him a light shove and he races off to procure his next sugar fix.

As I'm debating whether to treat myself, Trisha appears at my side and links her arm through mine.

"There you are," she says, "where's Vince?"

"In the agricultural building with my parents." I glimpse the Tupperware container in her left hand. "I thought you couldn't bring outside food into the fairgrounds."

"Fair food is *way* too bland for my Jamaican palate. Besides, mom says it's a good way to save money."

Trisha drags me toward a picnic bench and sits down. I scope out the crowd, taking in the familiar sights and sounds and trying not to let my thoughts wander to Jayden. He still hasn't called, but it doesn't mean anything. When he took me up on the Ferris Wheel and called it the highlight of his life, *that* meant something, and always will.

"So," Trisha says, "what's the latest on Mr. Perfect?"

Vince. She's talking about Vince. Obviously. "He's a Shakespeare nerd, but he won't help me with my essay on *Macbeth*. And he's really handy with car stuff. He changed the tires on the spare truck and fixed the tractor this week." I roll my eyes. "So annoying."

"You should give me his number. My uncle's been on the hunt for someone to fix his dying Impala for *months*."

"Vince doesn't carry a phone. And dad keeps him busy enough as it is."

"Oh, I get it," Trisha taunts, picking at a semi-congealed lump of curry chicken with a fork. "You don't want to give him up. So much for he's not your type, huh?"

"He's not. I'm just telling it like it is."

She laughs. "Whatever, Gabby."

"What is with you and all this lovey-dovey stuff? Vince is an acquaintance, not some long-lost heartthrob."

"He's got a crush on you."

"No, he doesn't!"

"No? Then why is he staring at you?"

I turn around. Across the midway, I spot Vince. He's wearing a brown coat, beige pants, and his old sneakers. The wind is messing up his hair—not disastrously, but enough to compel him to reach up and smooth it down, like he's self-conscious or something. And yes, he's looking straight at me.

I face Trisha again and shrug. "Probably just looking for somewhere to sit."

"Does he know about Jayden yet?"

"What do you think?"

Vince walks over to us, looks from me to Trisha, and asks, "Is this seat taken?" while nodding at the empty space on my left.

"Gabby was saving it for you," Trisha says with a smirk at me. "Isn't that nice of her?"

I motion to the bench, indicating that he can take a seat. He's brought a carton of fries, and I hate that the smell of them makes me hungry.

As if sensing this, Vince places them beside me—a peace offering. "I saw Ryan in the midway. Is he allowed to be off by himself?"

"I'm hoping the fairies come and take him away," I say. "Where've you been all this time?"

"I've been shadowing your father and making conversation with the exhibitors. Earlier today, I met a gentleman who'd be kind enough to take all that scrap metal in the shed off your hands. He assembles artwork from the loose pieces he acquires from local farmers' equipment."

Vince pulls a small, white business card out of the breast pocket of his coat and passes it to me.

"So, let me get this straight," I say. "He buys the junk off us, then turns around and sells it for even more? What do we get out of this?"

"A lot more floorspace."

I slip the card into my purse. "Thanks. Dad's gonna be thrilled."

Trisha flicks her eyes between us before something behind me catches her attention.

"Gabby, check it out. Isn't that Melanie Hargrave, from the volleyball team?"

I turn around. "I guess."

"I'm gonna go say hi to her. See you around, Vince." Trisha scoops up her lunch and dashes off.

He waves goodbye to her before turning back to me.

"Sorry about that. She likes to run off every now and then." I tuck some hair behind my ear.

"No harm done." Vince helps himself to a fry and takes a bite off the end. "So, how do you like being a farmer?"

"You mean a farmer's daughter? I don't mind it. But as soon as I graduate, I'm leaving this town and moving to the city." I ask him, "How do you like being a hired hand?"

"I love it. But I've always wanted to live in the country where it's quiet." Vince nudges the fries a bit closer to me until I eventually cave and take one. They're warm and fluffy on the inside, salty and crispy on the outside. The perfect treat on this cool afternoon.

We watch the crowd for a bit, silently judging the young families. The parents look miserable, and the kids are screaming their heads off, being revved up on sugar and fatty foods. I don't know where Vince got the idea that country equals peace and quiet, because I can barely hear myself think right now.

"Can I ask you something?" I say. I have to yell a bit, but Vince seems to catch every word. "When you first came here, you said your family obeyed a strict etiquette. Does that mean you never disagreed on anything?"

"We disagreed about a lot of things," he admits, which surprises me. "I may have been exaggerating somewhat when I said they were a peaceful, mannerly bunch."

"What kinds of things?"

"The usual: bedtimes, who gets to watch what on TV, whether or not I should move out of the house."

"One of those things is not like the other," I point out.

He hunches his shoulders, looks across the sizzling midway and kid-friendly rides, and explains, "I was needed to look after the younger ones. Eventually, it was my stepdad who convinced my mom this experience would be beneficial to me. He's always been the more diplomatic parent, though."

"I see."

Mom and dad soon join us, with Ryan in tow. He's halfway through a bag of cotton candy and gazing around wildly for another opportunity to break stuff or throw something. I reach across the table and help myself to a pinch of the sweet, strawberry-flavoured cloud, making him squeal in protest.

"Ryan," dad says in the deadpan tone of a parent who's fighting a losing battle.

"She took my cotton candy!"

"Technically, I paid for it." I tear off another hunk, looking to Vince. "Did you want some?"

"No, thank you."

"So, how are you enjoying the fair?" mom asks him.

"Greatly. Food, fresh air, good company. What more could a guy want?"

"Vince picked up a business card for you," I tell my parents—well, mainly dad. "He met a guy who buys scrap metal from local farmers and turns it into artwork, or something like that."

"I informed him that you were looking to clean out your driveshed, and he invited you to give him a call. It's on the card—"

I open my purse to retrieve the information. Dad squints at the tiny numbers on the back as I say, "Now you'll have tons of extra room to park the tractor you never let me drive."

"You don't know how to drive the tractor," mom reminds me. "You've never wanted to learn."

Naturally, she'd say this in front of Vince, Mr. Everything-is-a-learning-experience.

"Maybe I can teach you," Vince offers. "If it's okay with your parents, of course."

It's fine with them. Perfect, in fact. Ryan's getting antsy, so mom and dad escort him to the stall with the bottle smash game so he can blow off some steam, leaving Vince and I alone again.

"So it's settled," Vince says. "Saturday morning, after I've finished with my own responsibilities?"

"Saturday morning," I say. "It's a date."

Chapter 6

A week later, I'm in the middle of doing homework when Vince's footsteps creak up the stairs. This morning, I received my first tractor driving lesson. The controls are pretty much the same as the ones in a car, with a few crucial differences. First of all, a car doesn't come with any special attachments, like a bucket for carting around manure. Secondly, tractors are way louder, meaning Vince had to sit close in order to be heard. Really, really close.

He picks up his sketchbook and fans through the pages. Sometimes, after dinner, he sits on the porch and draws the world the way he sees it: in black and white. His subjects vary widely, from trees to watering cans and even my mother savouring a cup of coffee—anything that remains still long enough for him to obtain a preliminary contour. The rest he composes from memory, right down to the last grey splinter of wood. To see the world like that, to notice so much about things that receive so little thought… well, it makes you wonder how something like a kitchen table could go unnoticed.

He places the book beside me on my desk. "It's not complete yet," he says.

I shut my laptop and study the black and white image of our farmhouse, partially smothered by trees. He's even drawn the rocking chair and wind chimes, hanging by a rusted chain in the corner of the veranda.

"Looks finished to me," I say.

"Really? I haven't forgotten anything?"

"I doubt it. You have a better eye for that kind of stuff, anyway."

Vince nods and picks up his pencil. In the lower right-hand corner of the page, he signs his name, tying it together so that the y on the end of McCarthy underlines everything.

"What are you working on?" he asks.

"A lit report for my English class," I respond. "You know, pointless stuff."

"Did you try adding quotations?"

"It's out of the question. I need at least thirty." I hand him *Macbeth*. "I'm supposed to write about how the characters in the play represent 'the human condition.' Pathetic, right?"

Vince nods. His approval surprises me.

"So… can you give me a hand?" I ask.

He thumbs through the pages. "Could I borrow your chair for a minute?"

I let him sit down. He opens the computer and my document, then types rapidly, his fingers breezing over the keys. "Don't tell anyone I'm doing this, all right?"

"What ever happened to doing it myself—you know, so I could learn something?"

"Gabby, that was physics. Fully black and white. But English is so subjective that I doubt my input is going to detract from your education."

"Makes sense to me."

He keeps typing.

"You're a better writer than me," I whine. "My teacher will totally be able to tell the difference."

"That's why I'm simply extracting a verse, word for word. It should give you a starting point."

I read over his shoulder: *Life's but a walking shadow, a poor player / That struts and frets his hour upon the stage / And then is heard no more.*

"Chew on that for a while," Vince says, giving me back my chair.

"I don't get it. What does it mean?"

"It's not too challenging for you, is it?"

"It's *Shakespeare*," I say. "I might as well learn Mandarin."

I can feel Vince breathing down my neck as I type, sculpting meaning from the words he's presented. *Life's but a walking shadow.*

"It's intangible," I blurt.

"What is?"

"Life. You can't touch it, just like you can't touch a shadow."

"Now you're getting somewhere." He tucks his sketchbook under his arm and retreats to his half of the attic, giving me space to work.

I write a few paragraphs, then delete everything to start fresh. Without a comparable experience in which to anchor my understanding of the text, *Macbeth* is just a pile of words written by a long-dead playwright. It has no relevance to today's problems. Why do we spend so many hours of our life in school only to graduate with no practical skills?

I shut my computer again. Turning toward the wall, and Vince, I say, "Can I ask you something?"

"Sure. I can't promise an answer, though."

"Were you popular in high school?"

"Depends whom you ask."

Pushing back my chair, I approach the wall and peer around the corner. Vince is sitting on his bed, huddled over the sketchbook like it's some big secret. His pencil drifts across the page, barely marking the paper. "I'm asking you," I say at last.

He raises his gaze to mine, uncomprehending, then lets it fall back to the sketchbook. I'm sure the lines he's drawing mean something—like the lines in *Macbeth* are supposed to mean something—but I don't see it. All I see is a boy with a scar on his hairline who would be super cute if he weren't insufferably nerdy.

"Define 'popular,'" Vince prompts.

"Liked by everyone."

"No one is universally likeable."

"So, is that a no?"

"Why do you want to know?" He closes the sketchbook and sets it on his nightstand.

"I don't know. I just do."

A wave of warm, humid air reaches through the open window, rustling the pictures tacked to the corkboard above my bed. Vince and I moved the manure pile this morning, as part of my crash-course in daily farm management, so dad's had to find other, less noisy ways to occupy himself.

"I had a couple of good friends," Vince tells me. "But as for popularity, well, I've never considered the opinions of a bunch of teenagers to hold much value." His face pinches with regret. "That did not come out the way I'd hoped."

"It's okay." I smirk. "So you were the teacher's pet then?"

"In a word, yes."

"Big surprise."

He furrows his brows. "What's that supposed to mean?"

"Uh, I think it's pretty clear." Confusion registers on his face, forcing me to add, "You're perfect. You know a lot about a lot of things. You're polite and respectful. And you like school."

"I'm not perfect, Gabby. I have my strengths, but so do you. Lots of them, I'm sure."

"Right," I say, crossing my arms. "Because knowing how to take a cow's temperature is going to get me really far in life."

"You never know."

"I don't want to be a vet. Besides, it's way out of my league, including financially."

Vince puts the pencil back in the narrow tin box with the others and snaps it shut. "Mind if I ask what you *are* planning to do, instead?"

"Mom wants me to be a fitness instructor. She's already started researching kinesiology programs. She'll never let me quit swimming, even if I'm old and crippled up."

"That's pretty lofty."

"Maybe."

"Is that what you want, too?"

My eyes stray to the photograph in the corner of my desk. I'm standing in my one-piece swimsuit in front of the pool with mom and dad supporting me on both sides. Tanya is beaming with pride in the background, and Ryan is trying hopelessly to not look sour about my victory. Above the image, pegged on a nail in the beam, hangs my first medal—a bronze. I lift it off the nail and hand it to Vince.

"I got this when I was fifteen. Tanya made me train so much I couldn't lift a bucket of water for a week after the competition."

"I thought you put an end to competing after your accident."

"I stopped competing *seriously*. This was the weekend my grandparents were in town. They live in Petawawa."

Vince traces the lettering on the metal disk. "They must've been so proud of you."

"I guess. But it's still a bronze."

"So? A bronze means you tried. That's worth being proud of, in my absolutely worthless opinion."

I replace the metal. It waves back and forth for a moment before coming to rest against the wooden surface with a faint tap.

Vince points at my computer. "I'm distracting you."

"Not really."

"That paper's not going to write itself. If I were you, I would keep at it."

"If you were me, you wouldn't want anything to do with Shakespeare, *Macbeth*, or this pointless assignment."

"I should have been more specific. If I was in your *position*, I wouldn't procrastinate."

"I'm not procrastinating."

"No. You're just delaying the process."

"I'm *thinking*."

Vince raises a brow. "I bet you aren't."

"You know," I say, turning to look at him. "You just love to push my buttons. You're like a kid some days."

Vince pretends to jab some nonexistent buttons. "I'll leave you to it." He crosses the attic and descends the stairs, disappearing like a shadow in the dark.

Chapter 7

"Books away, everyone. We're starting off with a pop quiz this morning." The whole class groans. I pray for a miracle.

Mr. Berkley places a stack of quizzes on the first desk of each row and returns to the board as they make their way toward the back of the room. I take a sheet and move the dwindling stack along. I haven't updated my notes, much less studied, for a couple of weeks. I read the first question in silence:

Jimmy is travelling on his bicycle at 30km per hour. He sees a stop sign 150 meters away and begins to slow down when he is 30 meters from the sign. At the sign, he makes a full stop. Calculate his total travel time over the 150 meters leading up to the sign, his rate of deceleration, and average speed over the 150 meters.

There are four questions of this nature, and each one is increasingly challenging. I push my way through them, jot some random numbers so it looks like I tried, and turn it in. My stomach is churning the whole time in the way that it does right before a swim meet. Deep breathing only kind of helps. At least when I'm in the water, I know what to do.

Mr. Berkley walks us through some of Newton's Laws and leaves us to our devices while he grades the tests. I pick mine up on the way out the door. It's exactly what I predicted it would be.

One time, mom took me to the doctor for my annual checkup. A lot of things were changing back then: Ryan was about to start junior kindergarten, my parents had just taken out a loan to buy the farm, and a few of the girls in my class had started "budding." So, naturally, she wasn't in a peaceful place. Stress has a magnifying effect on everything. Minor issues suddenly become insurmountable challenges when the brain is under pressure. And I guess mom thought she was trying to be helpful when she stared the doctor straight in the eyes and asked if I had ADHD.

It was a horrifying acronym. It sounded deadly to my ten-year-old ears, like HIV and AIDS. At one point, I think I passed out from holding my breath for so long. I thought about my first swimming lesson, how the water moved seemingly under its own power, how my body was both a brick and a feather in that giant, turquoise bath. Mom kept a tight hold on my hand, like she was scared I'd float away from her as soon as the doctor opened her mouth.

Dr. Dillon looked perplexed. On cue, mom rattled off a list of reasons why she thought I might've been "ADHD positive" (I didn't know much back then, but I knew that in a medical context, the word "positive" was never a good thing). I wasn't doing well in school, she said. Daydreamed incessantly. Ran around the house like I was being chased by a ghost. Stuff she'd probably Googled right there in the waiting room while I was debating whether to play with the Barbies or the Tonka Truck.

Dr. Dillon smiled, cutting her off mid-tirade. "If it'll help ease your mind, I can put you in touch with a child psychologist. But I don't think you have anything to worry about."

It's a fact universally acknowledged that telling a mother not to worry is the best way to guarantee she does precisely that. If mom wasn't already a ball of stress when we arrived, then hearing these words from a trusted source completed the transformation.

"But what if she does?" mom asked, frowning skeptically. "All those things I listed—do they sound normal to you?"

"Normal is relative," Dr. Dillon assured her. "Gabby is growing up. Kids struggle a lot at this age."

"But what about—"

"Mrs. O'Connor. I promise, if anything is wrong, you will know."

Dr. Dillon sent us on our way. By some miracle, I managed to drag mom out of that office and down to the car, but I never forgot how being under the microscope made me feel. This is why I don't want to compete again. Why it bothers me when Vince watches. Deep down, I wonder if mom knows something I don't—if you can know something without really knowing it.

Trisha is chatting with Carla and Elaine a few lockers down from mine. She's pontificating about the radiation hazards associated with excessive cell phone use and how we shouldn't be zapping our brain cells on the daily. Such irony, coming from her.

She waves. "How'd you do?"

I hand her the paper. "Berkley thinks I'm an idiot."

"Did he say that?"

"No, but you can see it in his eyes."

Carla says, "It's not *that* hard. And anyway, he's always in his office after class. You should talk to him."

"I don't even know what he wants me to say."

"'I need help' would be a good start."

I switch my books and throw some retractable ballpoint pens into my bag. "I'm not *you*, Carla. You've got a knack for math. I don't."

"She's right," Trisha says. "Why don't you pitch in some time?"

"Sorry, can't. I've got dressage lessons four times a week plus my part-time job at the ice cream parlor."

Trisha drums her fingers on her chin, studying me. "Why don't you ask Vince?"

"Who's Vince?" Elaine asks.

"Gabby's new boyfriend."

"He's *not* my boyfriend." I snap the lock onto my door and sling my bag over my shoulder.

"He wants to be."

"No way."

"Yeah." Trisha turns to the other two girls. "Gabby likes him. It's just taking her a while to admit it."

"The reason it's taking so long," I say, gritting my teeth, "is because I don't have feelings for him, even though none of you seem to believe it."

"Well, *duh*," Trisha says. "Every time I drop by you're stuck on him like glue."

"You mean he's stuck on *me*. You don't know Vince. He's always all over me like a dirty shirt." The bell sounds as I back away from the group. "I've got to go."

"Call me," Trisha cries as I join the stream of bodies bobbing down the hall. "I want to hear everything!"

Everything. How typical of her to speak in such hyperbolic terms. I've already told her 'everything' there is to know about Vince: he's the perfect guest, a model citizen, the poster boy for good parenting. He knows tractors and tools and his way around a kitchen. I, on the other hand, can crawl from one end of the pool to the other in under a minute and stand at the end of the highest diving board without getting dizzy. My skills are as useful in my environment as Vince's glasses are for nocturnal vision.

I drag my feet through my afternoon classes: Home Economy, Mathematical Functions (which I abhor almost as much as Physics, but way less than doing my brother's laundry), and Exercise Science, which I was supposed to take next year had it not been for mom's squabble with administrators over my future vocation. Knowing this, I can only imagine what she must have in mind for grade twelve.

The truth is, I've never asked mom why she wants me to be a fitness instructor. Maybe she likes the ring to the words, or the reaction people have when she tells them her daughter's going to be featured in one of those fitness DVDs everyone rushes out to buy at New Year's. I have no issues with her embellishments though. As long as I don't have to work with thermodynamics or conduction, any stream of work sits well with me.

When I explain this to Vince after school, he insults me.

"You're a doormat, Gabby."

"A *what?*"

"A doormat. You let people trample you. What happened to grabbing the bull by the horns and deciding your own future?"

"Oh, please, everyone knows you can't control what happens to you."

Vince stacks the clean plates and tucks them in the cupboard above the sink. "No, but you can at least try to lay the framework for a life you would be moderately satisfied by."

I roll my eyes. Outside, a few yellow leaves flutter to the ground, landing silently on the porch.

"I have no problem teaching people how to exercise. I'll be helping to reverse the obesity pandemic."

"You mean epidemic?"

"Whatever."

Vince scoffs. He sorts some spoons and forks and slides them into the drawer.

"It's hard work," I say.

"I never said it wasn't. The point I'm trying to make is that it will be even harder if you're not passionate about it."

"I *am* passionate. It's great for stress therapy. Do you have any idea how many toxins you can expel through sweating?"

"A lot?" he replies, almost sarcastically.

"Exactly."

My cell phone buzzes on the table. Vince and I glance simultaneously at the device, and I catch a diabolical glint in his eyes. We both lunge for the phone.

"Vince!" I explode. "What are you doing? Give it back!"

He turns his back to me. "I'm just looking, Gabby."

"Vince, don't," I say. "Please."

"Why? What are you hiding?"

"Nothing."

"So? I'll only be a minute."

I peer over Vince's shoulder to see a text from Trisha.

When were you going to call me? she asks.

Vince's fingers move swiftly over the tiny keypad. "Mind if I reply?"

"Be kind to her," I warn. "She has a whole entourage. If you piss her off, they'll hunt you down."

"Kind to her? You mean kinder than you are?"

I could smack him.

Vince writes: *This is Vince M.*

A few seconds pass.

How are ya? :)

Vince looks at me. "How should I respond?"

"I don't know. You're the genius here, not me."

He nods, contemplating a reply. Then he answers: *Better now that Gabby's home.*

You two are adorable. Gabby doesn't think there's anything going on between you two, but I'm the expert and she's wrong, Trisha brags. *So are you guys dating or??*

"No," I say. "Tell her no."

"Hmm… what's your definition of 'dating'?"

I think about Jayden: the warm weight of his hand on my thigh, double-straws in an ice-cold Coke, frittering away hours on the phone, wanting to have the last word, the final *I love you.*

"What's yours?" I ask.

"Some quality alone time, a bit of intimacy. But mostly I equate dating with discovering a sense of unity with the other person."

"So, no dinner and movie?"

"Too traditional."

"Oh."

Vince replies: *We're working up to it.*

Aww, Trisha says.

"You know what," I tell him, stealing the phone from his hands. "Let's stop this. She makes me kind of crazy after a while."

"I thought she was your best friend."

"She is. But even the people you care about can get under your skin."

Vince rubs his chin. "Can it work in reverse? Can you care about someone who irritates you?"

"Define 'care.'"

Vince looks out the window momentarily, as if the right words might suddenly blow toward us. Come to think of it, I can't imagine Vince having a girlfriend. That's not to say he isn't capable of being in a relationship, but how is anyone supposed to live up to the ultra-high standards he's set for himself?

"Listening," he says after some thought. "That's what caring means to me: being able to listen to someone and understand them on a deeply personal level." Vince studies me. "What does it mean to you?"

"I don't know. Hanging out, I guess."

This is the wrong answer, just like whatever I wrote on my physics test was dead wrong. But in both cases, I'm at a loss for what to say.

Vince points at my phone. "So, how long have you been addicted to texting?"

"Forever. I've had a phone since I was twelve, but back then it was strictly for emergencies."

Vince nods. "And now?"

"Now it's attached to me constantly, as you can see."

"Even at school?"

"*Especially* at school. Mostly in physics."

"How are you doing in that class?" he asks. I can tell from the intonation of his voice that he's been spending too much time with dad. He's concerned, but not nearly as concerned as mom was that day at the doctor's. And it's still too much, especially after all that stuff he said about caring.

I roll my eyes, walk over to my bag, and pull out the test. "You tell me."

He studies the paper. "You're proud of this?"

"No. Of course not."

"The first question is so easy, Gabby."

"Prove it."

Vince reaches for a pen. He does a rough sketch of a street and a cyclist, jots some numbers here and there, and flies through the problem faster than I can translate it into meaning.

He circles the answer and passes it back to me. "This is where you should have arrived."

"I didn't even know where to *start*, let alone end."

"I can tell. Would you like some advice?"

"No."

"Take notes. Study weekly. It's a simple science."

"I hate notes. And I hate wasting my time on crap that won't benefit me in life."

Vince furrows his brows. "I thought you said a few minutes ago that no one can foretell what happens to them. This applies too, doesn't it?"

"We're done here."

"Let me help you," he says.

"I don't need your help."

"It won't cost you anything, but you'll appreciate the gains. It's a win-win situation."

Win-win. I wonder what's in it for him. "Maybe."

Vince holds out his hand to me. A question lingers in his gaze. Okay, maybe he's not terrible to look at, and those glasses can make even the most reluctant student care about their grades. "I want to show you something," he says softly.

I stick out my arm, placing my hand lightly in his. His fingers are warm. It's… kind of nice to be touched so gently, especially after not hearing from Jayden in so long.

Jayden. The thought makes me yank my hand back like I've been burned.

Vince leads me to the attic, this time without touching me at all. I hang back at the top of the stairs while he drags his suitcase out from under his bed and unzips it. Inside are a couple of books, *Astrophysics* and *Practical Applications in Optics*, which are nestled amongst some sweaters and a few pairs of pants. He pulls out a black binder and hands it to me.

"What's this?" I ask.

"It's the very rough draft of a book I started writing before I left home—a nonfiction book about physics, math, and science. My plan is to publish it with an academic press and distribute it to high schools across the province."

I turn the pages carefully, as if they might disintegrate in my hands. "Where did you learn all this, Vince?"

"Hours and hours spent at the public library. The way I consume physics and math isn't like how most young adults do. If you ask me, the texts given out in school aren't conducive to early adolescent minds."

"You're telling me." I close the binder. "So… why are you giving me this?"

"I'm lending it to you. You're welcome to borrow some of my ideas if you think they'll improve your own understanding."

"So you've been hiding this encyclopedia all along, and you didn't tell me? You could've spared me a lot of embarrassment today."

"I wasn't aware you were struggling so much until a few minutes ago."

"What else are you hiding?"

"Excuse me?"

I bite my lip. I don't know Vince, not really. For all I know, he could be a millionaire. He stares quizzically at my face, and I wonder if my expression is blank or concerned.

"All I mean is…" My voice fades into the musty attic air. I smile. "If you're writing a book on how to decode Shakespeare, you better come clean."

"Oh." He laughs, easing the tension between us. "Maybe in the future, but not right now. I still need to type all this up." Vince gestures to the binder, nestled safely in my elbow.

A door creaks downstairs. I hear mom first, hollering something I don't catch, followed by the crinkle of paper bags as she unpacks the groceries.

"I better go lend a hand, before we have clementines under the fridge again," Vince says, turning toward the stairs.

"Vince?"

He turns back, his hand wrapped around the wooden railing.

"Thanks. It really means something to me," I say.

"And what is that something?"

"Not having to spend lunch hours with my crusty old physics teacher. And now I might actually have a decent GPA, thanks to you."

Vince blushes a little. "Don't mention it. I'm here for you, Gabby." He turns away and leaves me standing at the top of the stairs.

A tiny vibration tickles my back pocket.

Wanna go out for pizza? :) Trisha writes.

I type: *Maybe another time.*

Why??

Vince and mom are conversing in the kitchen. I think Vince is cracking jokes, but it's hard to tell from inside the roof.

I have to study tonight, I tell her.

Alright, you nerd. Try not to have too much fun without me.

I switch off the screen, hating myself for disappointing her. Then I put it in my desk drawer and join my family downstairs.

*

"And so you see, when a second body exerts force on a first body, both bodies act in opposite directions yet with equal magnitude…"

Mr. Berkley is droning on about Newton's Laws of Motion. The guy sitting next to me is mutilating his binder with the tip of his pen, while the girl on my right is picking at her chipped nail polish. I'm exhausted from staying up last night, copying Vince's notes. I have to hand it to him: the guy knows how to teach. Any profession in which he's able to impart knowledge to other people would suit him fine.

I open my book and fan through the pages of notes. Vince awoke a few times in the night, disturbed by the glow of my desk lamp.

"Gabby?" he called softly. "Are you still awake?"

"I'm almost done."

"That's what you said an hour ago." Then he added, "You don't have to educate yourself all in one night, you know."

"I know." I paused. "What's velocity again?"

"Speed with direction."

"Great." I went on writing as Vince drifted back to sleep. I could have stopped there, but for once, I was actually deriving some sort of pleasure from homework. *So this is what it must feel like to be Vince,* I thought. Five minutes later, I fell asleep at my desk, using the binder for a pillow.

I stop on one particular page. In the corner I've drawn a heart no bigger than the nail on my little finger, and I don't think it was for Jayden.

Vince, mom, and I had fun last night. She made spaghetti and meatballs for three, since dad and Ryan were at a hockey meet. Dad offered for Vince to tag along, but he declined, claiming that the closest he ever came to team sports was playing basketball with a few neighbors when he lived in Oshawa.

I didn't text Trisha any more after that. After a little persuasion on Vince's part, mom let us watch a movie by ourselves in the living room. Partway through the film, he slipped an arm behind my back and kept it there until the end credits. Neither of us mentioned it afterwards.

Mr. Berkley has moved on to real examples of Newton's Laws in action. Whenever I glance at him, I imagine Vince standing at the board, turning nonsense into a wealth of information.

I hope to get out of class unnoticed today, so I can call Vince and thank him profusely for the binder, but Trisha ambushes me before I can blend into the crowd.

"Tell me everything," she demands. "Now that you and Vince are dating."

"We're not. It's just wishful thinking on his part."

She gives me a crafty look. "And I'll bet you were standing right beside him the whole time he and I were chatting."

"So, what? I wanted to make sure he didn't slip up."

"Slip up? Keeping secrets are we, Gabby?"

I pull out a granola bar and begin walking down the hall toward my locker. "I don't know."

"You are a terrible liar, you know that?"

"I would think that's a good thing."

"Good if you're trying to get information out of you." She points at the snack. "Got another one of those by any chance?"

I give her a fruit bar—which I hate—just so she'll stop begging. "Can I ask you something?" she says between chews.

"Well, you're on a roll, so you might as well."

"You're not gonna like it."

"Try me."

She pockets the wrapper. "Do you have a crush on Vince?"

The doodle of the heart flashes to mind. "Absolutely not. Where do you come up with these crazy ideas?"

"You don't like him at all? Not even as a friend?" We're in the girl's bathroom now, so anything Trisha says bounces annoyingly off the stall doors.

"He's a nice guy, but he's not my type. You should know me better than this by now."

"He's more than nice. He's a total gentleman. Remember that day at the fair?"

"How could I forget? Ryan swindled me out of ten bucks."

"So, what do you like about Vince?"

"Well… he's smart, for one thing. He gave me this binder of notes he has from his own physics stuff and said I could use it to help me study."

"Look, if I were you, I would date this guy. He's the whole package—*and* he's obviously in love with you."

"You can't prove that. Just because…"

"Because?"

I ball up the paper towel I've been using to dry my hands and drop it in the overfilled receptacle. "Just because we held hands for two seconds doesn't mean he wants to be my boyfriend. He's only being nice because my parents are around."

Trisha picks up her bag as we leave the bathroom and navigate the halls and bodies. Once in the cafeteria, she addresses me again.

"I think you should open up a bit to him. Maybe he's just dying to go out with you but doesn't know how to ask. What if he screws it up?"

"I don't think Vince could screw anything up if he tried." Truth is, this *has* crossed my mind a few times. It's occurred to me all those instances I've caught his gaze at the dinner table. Those times he holds the door for me, I wonder what other doors are standing between us, begging to be opened. How the coffee tastes so much better when he pours it and asks if I want sugar. How little I've been thinking of Jayden.

"I think you should give him a chance," Trisha says, barging into my thoughts. "You might be pleasantly surprised."

"I already am."

Chapter 8

Two days later, Vince and I are chatting over coffee when Ryan comes barging into the kitchen waving a piece of paper.

"I passed!" he exclaims, shoving the test under Vince's nose. "I got a B, see? Now dad will let me watch as much TV as I want."

"Congratulations," Vince says. "I knew you had it in you."

"I did," Ryan beams, "the *whole* time."

"I think you owe someone a word of thanks," I say, stirring my coffee. "Obviously you weren't going to succeed on your own."

"Yes, I was."

"No, you weren't."

"Was *so*."

"Ryan, your math mark was taking a nosedive until Vince gave you some pointers. Admit it."

"No. I had it in me the whole time. See? I got a B."

Vince shakes his head. "Don't bother, Gabby. Maturity yields gratitude."

Ryan is puzzled. "What does that mean?"

"You don't have to thank me right now. But I'll expect one later."

I suppress a giggle at Vince's remark as my brother, still pondering the meaning of this statement, walks from the room with the test hanging at his side.

Vince rises to pour himself a second cup. "Kids, right?"

"I know. They're so annoying."

"And they have a lot to teach me."

"Teach *you*?" I make a face. "That's a first."

Vince turns away from the counter clutching mom's favourite mug in his hand. "Why?"

"I don't know if you've noticed, but you practically run this place."

He glances pointedly at the mug and smirks. "How am I doing?"

"You seem okay. I think mom and dad might keep you."

I glance at the toast crumbs on my plate. Vince had already made breakfast by the time I came in from feeding the cows. Before I headed out, I made sure to apply a few strokes of mascara and a couple swipes of lip gloss. Vince said the bits of hay in my hair were "a nice touch." Leave it up to him to turn anything into a compliment.

"So, you want to be a teacher?" I say, clearing the dishes from the table.

"Yes."

"Just any teacher?"

"Math or physics, I haven't decided yet."

"You have time."

He hesitates. "Funny you should say that, because there's something I've been meaning to talk to you about."

"What's that?"

"Well." Vince sighs. "I've been thinking about the future, about what I'm going to do after I finish working here." He waits, but I don't interrupt him. "I think you should know that I've applied to university."

"Oh."

"And if I get accepted," he continues, "I might need to make arrangements to stay with someone else."

"You can stay here as long as you want, Vince," I assure him. "It's okay. Mom and dad will keep paying you and we can keep sharing the attic. It's no big deal."

"It's not a local institution." Vince sets his coffee down on the counter. "It's in Washington."

"Washington, D.C.? Why? We have schools around here that offer decent programs, too."

"I've given it a lot of thought, and I really feel like American University is the place for me. And trust me, I've done copious research on this. It was AU, or Pennsylvania, but UPenn's more interested in astronomical concepts, which I adore, too, but not enough to want to pursue a career in it."

I ease myself into a chair, feeling shaky. "You're going away."

"Yes, but not for several months, Gabby."

"When did you apply?"

"Last week, while you were at school. I wanted to buy myself time to explain it to you, because I wasn't sure how you would handle the news." Vince reaches into the pantry and produces a pack of cookies. He opens the package and slides the tray out, setting the treats on the table. "I suppose this could have been worse."

"Worse, how?" I help myself to an Oreo and wrench the two halves apart.

"You could have been indifferent about it. I could have told you and you might have said 'whatever.'"

I hear Trisha's voice at the back of my mind. *He's obviously in love with you.* I look Vince in the eyes and catch a glimmer of sorrow. He's only doing what's best for him and his future after all.

"Does this bother you?" he asks.

"Kind of."

We're both quiet now. The kitchen is noisy in its emptiness—the faucet dripping, the clock ticking, the rusty jangle of the windchimes outside. Mom loves the silence; I don't. And I don't like how my heart is thumping in my chest, how Vince is staring at me, how I'm staring back.

Jayden. I make myself think of Jayden.

Vince swallows audibly, like they do in the movies. "So. Yeah. That's it."

"Okay." Like when Jayden said he loved me and I said *Okay*. Like it was no big deal, even normal to say goodbye for the last time. And maybe this is a good place to end things with Vince, when nothing is clear or sharp, when neither of us can get hurt.

After a second, I push my chair away from the table. The mascara was a stupid idea: all it does is get in my eyes. "I should go see if dad needs any help."

"And I should go check on Ryan."

"Okay."

"Okay." Vince smiles, puts the cookies back in the pantry, and tucks in his chair. I make myself look away as he leaves the room to go find my brother.

I step into the chill. My boots flap against my legs as I head up to the barn, wrapped in its misty shawl on the hill. Dad's got the door open for fresh air. The cows are in the pasture out back, splotches of white and black amidst the foxy brown of autumn. How could Vince ever leave this place? Leave *us*?

When I get closer, I can hear dad whistling. He always whistles when he works, like windchimes. I guess the cows find it soothing.

"Hey, dad," I say, crossing my arms over my open coat.

"Gabby," he replies, his voice high and bright in the stillness of the morning. "Everything okay?"

Okay. "Yeah. I just wanted to see if you needed any help."

"I could always use some help. Where's Vince?"

"In the house helping Ryan with homework." I follow dad down the aisle as he goes on checking things off his clipboard. "Did he tell you he applied for university?"

The pen in dad's hand runs out of ink. He gives it another experimental scratch, then sticks it in the pocket of his overalls and pulls out a fresh one. His plaid jacket billows in the wind. "He did? Good for him."

"Yeah. It's great." I glance out at the field, with its huge metal feeder and sparse layer of trees, and of course, all the cows. Most of them are lying down, which allows them to ruminate and produce more milk.

Dad comes over to the fence where I'm standing and gives me a peculiar look. "Do you think you'd ever want to take over one day?"

"I don't know. I think maybe I'd like to go away for school." I rest my elbows on one of the fence boards. Everyone else I know is going somewhere: Vince is going to Washington, Jayden is probably going to some war-torn country, and even Trisha has talked about spending the year after graduation in Jamaica with her grandmother, who owns a grocery store near the beach.

"Ryan could always take over," I suggest, "he likes it here."

"Well, if he doesn't get his grades up, he might not have a choice." Dad adds, "I need to go into town for some supplies. Do you want to come?"

It beats sitting around here, ruminating over whether Vince will stay, and if not, what it's going to be like without him.

I turn away from the fence to lead the way to the truck. "Okay."

*

Dad and I get home later than expected, well past dinnertime. Darkness seeps into the earth; the cows still need to be brought in, but mom is in the kitchen and a car I don't recognize sits in the driveway.

He pulls up to the shed and turns off the engine. "You go on inside. If you see Vince, tell him it's time to bring in the herd."

"Okay." The passenger door creaks as I throw it open. I can't take my eyes off the car for some reason. It's a plain silver Honda Civic with a bumper sticker imploring tailgaters to 'Support Our Troops.' The license plate is rusty. We don't get many visitors out here, so this is cause for curiosity.

Dried mud sloughs off my boots as I climb the wooden steps and enter the house. But when I get inside, instead of mom's cooking or the fireplace, I smell Axe.

"Jayden."

He turns to me. It's only been a few months since he left, but he's completely transformed in that time. Well, everything except for his eyes. My breath catches in my throat as Jayden gets up from the table and his arms form a circle around me.

I breathe him in. He must've worn the Axe for me, for old time's sake. His arms remind me of the legs on a fancy wooden table, how they start out thick at the top and gradually return to normal proportions near his wrists. A buzzcut completes the image.

Jayden holds me at arm's length, as if I'm the one who's unrecognizable. "Wow," he says, "wow."

Wow, indeed. "What are you doing here?" I ask him.

Jayden looks surprised, but recovers swiftly. "I had a bit of time off and wanted to see you." He makes a sweeping motion with his arms. Even his chest could be made of solid oak.

Mom picks up her mug of tea, saying, "I'll go let Vince know it's time for evening chores."

"Right." I'd already forgotten about what I promised dad. Jayden is here, in my kitchen, looking like the lovechild of GI Joe and Edward Cullen. I think I need to sit down.

Slowly, the smile fades from Jayden's face. I guess he was expecting me to be more exuberant, more fan-girly, about his return. In a way, I think I expected that too.

He assumes the seat next to me and wraps his hand around mine. Now that the shock of seeing him is wearing off, I can feel the butterflies returning to my stomach. Appearances aside, Jayden hasn't changed a bit. He still knows I'm a sucker for those little knuckle massages he gives with his thumb. I give myself over to the feeling, even as I hear footsteps coming down the stairs.

"You look good, Gabby," Jayden says.

"So do you." I trace the bulge of his bicep as Vince enters the kitchen.

Jayden follows my gaze to the boy in the background. Vince looks like a spaghetti noodle compared to my army cadet boyfriend, but I find myself hoping he'll say something to break the awful tension in the air. Instead, Vince simply nods in acknowledgement, zips up his black sweater, pulls on the work boots dad lent him, and slips outside without introducing himself.

"Who's that?" Jayden asks, cocking a thumb at the door.

"Vince. He's the hired help."

"He lives in the house?"

"Yes." Now probably isn't the best time to mention my room, specifically. "He's okay. Mom and dad like him."

"Ah." It's the most ambiguous *ah* I've ever heard: I can't tell if he means *ah* as in *whatever* or *what does he mean to you?*

"So, how's RMC?" I ask, hoping he'll forget about Vince.

"Brutal. The days start at the butt crack of dawn and run really late. We run around a lot. You should see what they feed us."

I nod, even as my eyes are drifting to the window and Vince's receding silhouette. "That does sound like hell."

"But enough about me. What have you been up to?"

I almost say *waiting for you to call*, but that sounds too desperate, not to mention dishonest. "The usual: school, swimming, shoveling cow crap."

"Sounds like you need a night on the town."

"What did you have in mind?"

"Dinner and a movie? If you wanna do something else, that's cool too. I already cleared it with your mom."

"No, dinner and a movie is fine. But, um, I should probably shower and put on non-farm clothes."

"You do that, my sexy little farm girl. In the meantime, I'll be snooping through your pantry for a snack." Then Jayden leans forward and presses his lips to my cheek, drowning me in his scent.

I head upstairs to get ready for our date. As I wash my hair and reapply my makeup and pick out my outfit, all I can think about is how different things would be if I hadn't met Jayden. Maybe I'd be a better student: you see, when you're the girl who's dating the older guy, grades don't matter as much. Besides, that's not the thing most people focus on.

I'm stuck debating between two scarves when Vince comes upstairs. Now that the cows are all tucked in for the night, mom will surely put him to work cleaning the oven or alphabetizing her gardening books. He unzips his sweater and tosses it onto the bed as he disappears around the wall, apparently not noticing me.

Then he asks, "Who's the guy?"

"My boyfriend, Jayden."

"He seems nice."

Vince reappears wearing a light green t-shirt instead of the white one he went out in. To think he was changing only a few feet away, all while asking about my boyfriend… Maybe there's nothing going on between us, after all.

"Yeah." I grab the scarves off my bed and hold each one up to my throat. They're both tartan, except one's blue and the other's a deep, seductive red. It's been so long since Jayden and I went out and I don't want him to get the wrong idea about how I feel, which in this moment is a cocktail of excited and confused.

Vince is standing beside the wall when I say, "Jayden and I are going on a date, but I can't decide which scarf to wear—red or blue?"

I switch back and forth between them a couple of times, highlighting my indecision.

His eyes flicker from one to the other before finally coming to rest on my face. "Blue. It brings out your eyes."

Vince turns toward the stairs and is gone before I can thank him.

*

It doesn't take long for Jayden and I to fall back into our old routine. We stop at the local Mini Mart first, where we peruse the shelves full of chips, candy, soda, soap, instant rice, and magazines. The clerk keeps sizing Jayden up like he's not sure whether to call the cops or offer him a job as a security guard. After a bit more wandering around, I get a bottle of Minute Maid orange juice and a pack of Swiss Rolls, just like when we were in high school and cutting sixth period. As we stroll along Main Street eating our respective treats, Jayden tells me more about military school. Everything sounds hard there: the drills, the classes, the chores. He tells me about the guys—and girls—in his squadron and the co-ed showers on campus. Mostly, he's just happy to be back in *our neck of the woods*, like we're wild animals who eat with our hands and he's here to civilize us.

The movie's okay. Dinner is nice. I'm pretty sure the girl who serves us hates me for dating a living, breathing action figure, but I don't care. I'm used to people looking at me funny whenever Jayden is present. And, besides, I'm not really paying attention.

"So that guy," Jayden says, pulling my focus back from a poster of Marilyn Monroe. "Vince? What's his story?"

"He's been working for us for a couple of months. Since I'm in school during the day, dad needed someone who could help him around the farm. But he's not planning to stay forever."

"Good. I don't like the thought of some weirdo peeping on my girl when I'm not around."

Weirdo? Peeping? Those aren't words I think of when I picture Vince. "He's actually really nice, Jayden. And he doesn't peep."

"Ah, so he's gay."

"What? No."

"Are you sure?"

"I mean, I'm pretty sure. Not that it would be a problem if he was." Now I'm starting to remember all those things I didn't like about Jayden, like how generous he was with his opinions, and maybe I was drawn to that because I never particularly liked myself. But now? Now, I think maybe I'm enough—even without Jayden hanging on my arm like a glittery gold bracelet.

I pull my hand away and he instantly attempts to take it back. "Come on, Gabby. Don't be cold."

I stare at the leftovers on my plate, with their dull glaze of neglect, and feel a flash of white-hot anger ignite behind my eyes. "Don't tell me what to do."

"Wow." He holds up his hands, calling for a truce.

I take a deep breath. "Sorry. I guess I'm tired."

"It's fine." Jayden dunks the straw back into his Coke and slurps loudly.

And then it hits me. I can't believe I didn't see it before: Jayden didn't join the army out of some duty to his country. He did it because of how it makes him look, the way people fawn over his Ken doll body, the privilege of calling me *his girl*. Like I'm something he needs to protect with his life.

Fuck him.

"I'm not your girl," I mutter down to the table.

Jayden leans in like he didn't hear me. "What are you saying?"

"I'm not a toy that you can pick up and play with whenever you get bored," I say. My voice is shaking, but I soldier on. "You go weeks without calling me, then show up and make some big, romantic gesture thinking it'll make up for not being here? That might work on Barbie, but I have a brain, Jayden."

He's staring at me. His big, beautiful eyes are staring at me in a way they never have before, and that's how I know we're doomed.

The waitress comes over to our table and begins to clear away our plates. "Can I get you anything else?"

"Just the bill." After she leaves, Jayden gives me a slightly bewildered, hangdog look. "What are you saying?" he asks again.

"I'm saying…" My eyes are tearing up. "I think we should break up."

"Break up?"

I'm prepared for him to grab my hand this time and drag my fingers out of reach. For a moment, it occurs to me that doing this in public is only going to hurt me, not him: Jayden could storm out and leave me here, and I'd look like an idiot for letting him go.

"Gabby, you're not making any sense," Jayden whispers. "I thought you were happy to see me."

"I am. But we're different people now. You're in college and I'm…"

"Don't be silly. You're still my girl, even when we're hundreds of kilometers apart."

"I'm *not* your girl. Not anymore."

Jayden's eyes go wide. I think they even turn a little red around the edges. The girl arrives with our bill, and Jayden pays her in cash, tacking on a generous tip for good measure. I flinch when the coins clatter onto the wooden table.

We drive back to the farm in silence. A thick fog blankets the road. It's supposed to snow soon, but the chill in the air doesn't compare to the interior of the car. When we pull into the driveway, mom is in the kitchen washing dishes, the light above the barn is on, and the attic window is softly lit. The reality of breaking up with Jayden doesn't hit me until he lets out a breath and gently punches the steering wheel in frustration.

"Damn it, Gabs," he mutters. "I just don't—I don't understand. Did I do something?"

"No. It's me. I've changed."

"Yeah, you have." Jayden adds, "You're supposed to be happy for me. I'm finally doing something worthwhile."

"I am happy for you… but I'm not happy *with* you anymore." Saying it out loud is a relief and a shock. I used to think Jayden was perfect, until I met Vince.

He sets his jaw, looks down at his lap. He really is beautiful. I'm sure he'll make some girl very happy one day. But that girl won't be me.

I reach for the door and freeze. I'll never see those eyes again, so I turn toward the driver's seat and take them in one last time. "Good luck out there."

Jayden's mouth flexes into a lopsided smile. He leans forward and skims the back of his hand down my cheek in place of a goodbye kiss.

I've barely taken three steps toward the front door when his car peels out of the driveway. Just like that, there's no more Jayden. No more movie dates. No more Axe. I hurry into the house as the pressure in my chest builds, knowing only that I need to be alone.

"How was your date?" mom asks. I rush past her without giving an answer. My feet pound up the stairs to the second floor, then straight into the attic. I make it to the window in time to see Jayden's car speeding down the road, a stream of exhaust fumes trailing after him. The taillights grow dim and eventually fade from view. And then he's gone.

"Gabby?"

I turn away from the window and find Vince standing near the top of the stairs. Two months ago, if someone had told me I'd break up with Jayden for the boy in the attic, I wouldn't have believed them. But here I am, and my hands are shaking, and nothing makes sense until I walk over to Vince and wrap my arms around his shoulders. It takes him a second, but when he hugs me back, I know this was the right thing to do.

"You don't have to tell me anything," Vince whispers, "but if you need to talk, I'm here."

"I know." I disentangle myself from him. He fingers the blue scarf bunched around my neck, prompting me to say, "I never wear this one."

"So why did you?"

I shrug as our eyes meet. "I guess I felt it was time for a change."

Vince smiles. Downstairs, Ryan is haranguing mom for a snack. So, maybe not everything is changing, but this feels like a good place to start.

Chapter 9

When I was seven years old, my grandma on dad's side died of colon cancer. She'd been battling the disease for months, and dad would often have to take time off from work to shuttle her to and from the hospital. As she neared the end of her life, our house became suffused with death. After the funeral, everyone brought us flowers, presumably to restore the life that had been taken from our family.

But the flowers only suffered under our collective neglect, releasing the swampy stink of decay throughout the rooms they occupied. It was hard to watch them go like that, so beautiful one day, then brown and flaccid the next. It made me angry, seeing the mess their starving petals left behind. And I wondered: what was the point in watching something grow only to let it wither away so carelessly?

There are five stages of grief: denial, anger, bargaining, depression, and acceptance. When Jayden told me he was joining the military, I was determined not to believe it. I thought about all the white roses, slowly dying at the stems though they looked okay from afar, kind of like Grandma Hazel before the cancer took over her body. I tried to make him stay, promised to change if he changed his mind. But he went anyway, killing me in the process, until I was nothing but thorns.

Breaking up with Jayden wasn't like losing him the first time. The stages felt accelerated, especially the acceptance part. Deep down, I know breaking up was the right thing to do, even if it was painful.

At lunchtime, I sit at a table with Trisha, Carla, and Elaine, and try to act like everything is fine. Elaine is going on about her latest fixation: eligible bachelor Ethan Mackenzie. They have chemistry class together, and they're both straight-A students, so things are heating up between them—and not in a good way.

"You won't *believe* what happened in chemistry this morning," Elaine says. She picks up the clementine from her lunch tray, digs her nails into the rind, and spirals it off. "I told Mr. Meyers I wanted to complete my yeast catalase experiment by myself, but he said Ethan was already working with yeast and that we could" – she stops peeling the fruit in order to draw a pair of air quotes – "'share resources' by working together. I swear, if Ethan makes me do all the work, I'm going to denature *his* protein."

Carla nods. "The only group work I want to be a part of involves Zeus. At least he won't take all the credit." She reaches into her backpack for her phone. "Speaking of which, wanna see a picture?"

"Okay, new topic," Trisha interrupts. She jabs me with her plastic fork. "The boy in the attic."

"Is that legal?" Elaine wonders.

"I don't want to talk about it," I mumble.

Carla turns her phone toward us. She has about a million pictures of her horse, a smoky grey Hanoverian gelding named Zeus, and grabs any excuse to show him off. We admire the image just long enough to cleanse Ethan from our minds, then the focus shifts back to me.

"So, attic boy," Elaine says, separating the clementine segments.

"Vince," Trisha says, "Gabby's new boyfriend."

"He's not my boyfriend."

"Wait, what about Jayden?" Carla asks.

"Yeah, what happened to Jayden?" Trisha's eyes pop out of her head. "Oh, my god. Does Vince know about Jayden yet?"

"Of course he does." I glance down at the apple sauce I've been stirring. I couldn't eat breakfast this morning, even though Vince made pancakes with Nutella to cheer me up, and my appetite still eludes me.

"Okay, and?" Trisha is leaning so close to me I'm convinced she smells trouble.

"And…"

Elaine stops chewing. "Did something happen with you and Jayden?"

"Actually, yeah. We broke up."

"Are you for real?" Elaine asks.

"I had to do it. It's complicated," I add, waving my spoon.

"But it's Jayden Sommers," she argues.

"And?"

"And who the hell breaks up with Jayden Sommers?"

"Wait." Trisha grabs my arm. "Is this because of Vince?"

"I'm lost. Are we talking about Jayden, Vince, or the boy in the attic?" Carla asks.

"All of the above," Trisha snaps. "Now pay attention."

But I don't want their attention. I may have accepted that Jayden and I are over, but that doesn't mean I'm no longer upset about the breakup. And Vince… well, I'm still trying to figure out where he fits in to the picture.

I gather up my backpack and picked-over lunch and cut a beeline to the door. Trisha might follow me, but I'm in no mood to be interrogated today. The applesauce and turkey sandwich slide into the trash and I step into the hallway. About thirty seconds later, Trisha trots out of the cafeteria, her Jamaican flag keychain swinging wildly from her bag.

She slips on her beanie as we walk back to my locker. "I don't know why I ever left Jamaica. It's so damn cold in this country," she laments, wrapping her arms around herself. "So where are we going?"

"*I'm* not going anywhere," I say, "mom says I need to get my grades up. This is the year colleges start looking at transcripts. And before you ask, Vince has nothing to do with it."

"And he has nothing to do with you breaking up with Jayden, right?"

We reach my locker. I spin the combination lock until it pops open and swap out the books in my backpack, making sure I have everything I need for my afternoon classes. My sports bag, which contains my swim gear, is crammed onto the shelf above my coat. Tanya says I need to spend all my free time at the pool if I want to be ready for the competition. After everything that's happened with Jayden, I could use the extra post-workout endorphins.

Trisha pinches my arm. "*Hello.* Earth to Gabby."

"Sorry." I swing my backpack over my shoulder and close the door. "I'm a little bit distracted today."

"Are you at least going to tell me why you broke up with Jayden?"

"He's… different, Trish. He showed up at our house all brawny and clean-cut and… I don't know. Maybe I'm looking for something else. Something a little less clichéd."

Her dark brown eyes narrow on me. "You swear this has *nothing* to do with Vince?"

"I don't know! I've never dated a guy like Vince before. I have no idea how it's supposed to feel."

Trisha scoops up my hands, protecting me with her warm, gentle touch. She has her grandmother's smile, the kind that can make you see light at the end of even the darkest tunnels.

"It's supposed to feel like this," she says, indicating my hands, "safe."

As she lets go, she casts a disdainful look at the doors, where a bunch of jocks have returned from a snowball fight. Trisha shivers and stuffs her hands into her coat pockets before turning away from the traveling circus. "I should go. I promised mom I'd join study group, before someone mistakes my math grade for the temperature outside."

It isn't until Trisha leaves that I notice one of the guys by the door staring at me. I think his name is Casey. He's got that wintery glow and his dark blond hair is matted with wet snow. A smile reaches his ears and before I know it, he's crossing the busy hallway on a direct path to where I'm standing.

"Hey," Casey says, running a hand through his hair.

"Hey," I say back. "Casey, right?"

"Yeah. I used to be friends with Jayden." He adds, "I heard he's back in town."

"He's just visiting for a few days. Actually, I think he went home last night." After how badly I humiliated him at the restaurant, I can't imagine Jayden would have had cause to linger, what with the town being so small and the locals being so chatty.

Casey nods. "Well, if you're not doing anything later, maybe we can hang out. I don't think Jayden would be mad."

No, I don't think he would. But Vince might.

"I can't. I have swim practice after school." I hike up my backpack, trying to give the impression that I'm a studious person and in a hurry to get to the library, instead of the girl who attracts senior guys like a magnet. "Sorry."

"It's cool." Casey turns away, his blue and yellow ski jacket blending back into the crowd. "See you around, Gabby."

"Bye, Casey."

His friends are laughing when he rejoins the group, like Jayden's friends did that day he asked me out. Then Casey glances back at me, teeth bared in a grin. I spin on my heel and weave through the bodies clogging up the hall, dodging a few curious gazes as I head for the library to work on my English paper. I can still hear Casey's friends laughing as I turn the corner.

✳

From the moment the water touches my skin, I feel weightless, freed from the pain of the last few days. I dive deep into the pool, propelling myself forward with a series of dolphin kicks before slicing through the surface of the water for air. Tanya is standing at the finish line, armed with a stopwatch and a clipboard. Her white shorts are all I can see as I grab the edge of the pool and haul myself out.

"Forty-seven-point-three seconds," she says as I slip off my goggles. "Not your best time."

"I know." A chill prickles my wet skin. In other lanes, other swimmers are practicing their breast strokes and butterflies, lurching through the chlorinated water with grace and power. Any of them could easily beat me at the 50-meter freestyle.

As if divining my thoughts, Tanya chirps, "On the flip side, your technique is rock solid. And you know what happens to rocks when you throw them into a pool?"

"They sink."

"Exactly." She resets the timer. "Let's try this one more time. And remember: lots of energy coming off the block."

I reel my feet out of the water and walk to the opposite end of the pool. Climbing back onto the block, I pull my goggles down over my eyes and shake the nerves from my fingertips. The water is clear and calm before me. I wrap the toes of my left foot around the front of the stumpy, black board and brace my arms at my sides.

On Tanya's signal, I spring from my perch and glide into the opalescent depths. The sounds of the fitness complex are suddenly reduced to a dull hum, but a few seconds later they come rushing back, and so does the supply of oxygen. I bring my arms out of the water in an alternating pinwheel motion and kick with my legs. I have to break thirty-five seconds if I want to stand a fair shot at winning. As Tanya draws nearer, my lungs begin to burn with effort. By the time I reach her, I'm completely out of breath.

Tanya glimpses the watch and sets her jaw.

"Well?" I prompt.

"Fifty-point-eight." She shakes her head. "Normally, practice makes people faster, but your times are all over the place. Are you breathing like I taught you?"

"Most of the time."

"What's going on, Gabby?"

I'm hanging on the edge of the pool, trying to keep my shoulders submerged so the rest of my body doesn't shake. "What do you mean?"

Tanya directs a pointed look at Vince, sitting in a plastic chair near the changerooms. I can't tell if he's smiling from all the way over here, but he's definitely watching.

"Boy trouble?" Tanya intones.

"Vince is innocent. I swear."

"Then why are you swimming like you have a bag of rocks tied to your feet?"

"I don't know. I guess I'm a bit distracted tonight. I broke up with my boyfriend on the weekend—"

"Blah, blah, blah, excuses, excuses. Look, Gabby, I'm your coach, not your girlfriend. I'm here to help you train and get better times. So, you can either focus on boys or you can get your head in the game and swim like your life depends on it." She arches her reddish-blonde brows. "Hmm? What's it going to be?"

Of course, the correct answer is b) get my head in the game, because that's what mom and dad keep paying for. I'm exhausted and my muscles hurt, but I can't quit now, or Jayden will have surely won.

"Last one," Tanya instructs, "and this time, aim for thirty-five or under."

So I drag myself out of the water and march defiantly toward the block, motivated by spite rather than a passion for the sport.

I climb up on the platform and face my reflection one last time. *Become the water.* That's what mom used to say when I was first learning to swim. I always tried so hard to fight it, to keep my limbs in permanent motion until every drop of energy was drained from my body. But tonight, I choose to surrender. I let Jayden enter my mind and pass through without resistance. I let Casey and his idiot friends glide over my conscience. In no time at all, my thoughts are clear and I am ready.

I enter the pool like a dart, cutting deep, traveling low and fast for about fifteen yards until I rise for air. I bring my elbows high over my head, pushing the water behind me with each stroke. I concentrate on the air at the back of my throat, on drawing in more than I put out. Every couple of seconds, Vince flashes into view—and this time, I can tell from the angle of his mouth that nothing is weighing me down.

I reach the end of the lane and beam up at Tanya. "Well?"

"Forty-three."

"That's good. Better than last time."

"Something's still holding you back. Whatever it is, please get rid of it ASAP." She checks her watch, then says, "Our time's up for tonight. Hit the showers. I'll work on your new training schedule and see where we can improve."

"Okay."

As she walks away to check on another student, Vince strides toward the edge of the pool and smiles tentatively. I pretend to rub the water out of my eyes to hide their pinkish tinge.

"You were amazing," he says. The light from the pool dances over his face in streams of whitish-blue.

"I'm too slow."

"Says who?"

"My coach. Were you even listening? I have to break thirty-five seconds if I want to win the 50-meter freestyle."

I brace myself for another one of Vince's trademark lectures, but he refrains from speaking, as if he knows I already have enough on my mind. Instead, he offers his hand to help me out of the pool. I reach for my towel and twirl it around my shoulders as the water cascades off my body, leaving a trail of wet footprints behind me.

"You seemed pretty good to me," he says after a minute or two, "as I said, I'm no expert, but my opinions are sincere."

"I know." I glimpse Vince's face. "I'm sorry."

"It's okay. We all have bad days."

I peel off my swim cap, unleashing my thick, black curls from its silicone grip. Vince follows me as far as the ladies showers before saying, "I know it's none of my business, but your less-than-optimal performance wouldn't have anything to do with the guy who visited on the weekend, would it?"

I turn away from the door. The towel's damp weight soaks into my skin, making me chilled and uncomfortable.

Finally, I say, "I didn't like the way he talked to me. We met when I was fifteen, and back then I liked thinking I belonged to someone. But I'm not that girl anymore, and I didn't want him weighing me down."

The blue of the water on Vince's skin brings out his eyes. "Did you love him?"

The chemical-laden air catches in my throat. I somehow manage to squeak, "Define 'love.'"

"Were you two just hanging out? Or was there something more?"

"It's getting late. I should get dressed…"

He nods, his expression unreadable. "I'll wait for you in the truck."

And wait he does. I linger in the changerooms, buying myself time to formulate a proper answer. If love means wanting the other person to be happy, then it's true that I loved Jayden. A microscopic part of me thinks I still might, despite knowing I deserve more than someone who treats me like a cherished object. But I can't say any of this to Vince, because after everything he's done for our family, I want him to be happy, too.

The ground is covered in a sprinkle of snow when we leave the fitness complex. We arrive home about fifteen minutes later, and through the smoky darkness I spot dad on the path to the barn, talking to someone I don't immediately recognize. We pull into the driveshed and get out of the truck, saying nothing to each other as we make our way toward the silhouettes.

"Ah, there you are, boy." It's our neighbour, Rick, dressed in a hefty brown coat, denim overalls, and his favourite ball cap. His eyes ricochet off my face, like he's not quite sure how to address me.

"Your mother called," Rick continues, unwilling to let my presence stand in the way of important business. "She wants to know if everything is okay."

Vince slips into a state of practiced politeness, although his face appears more strained than usual. Rick is the closest thing he has to family out here, but their interaction feels better suited to strangers on a bus. "Everything's fine, Uncle Rick."

"Yeah?" He doesn't seem convinced, and frankly, neither am I. "She's getting worried. She thinks you might be…"

Rick doesn't get a chance to finish this thought, though, because suddenly Vince's voice snaps like an icy tree branch, startling us all. "I said I'm fine. Tell her to stop worrying."

Dad looks at me with his eyebrows slightly raised. "Gabby, why don't you see if your mother needs any help in the house?" And because I'm still speechless from Vince's outburst, I simply nod and do as he says.

I head down to the house and jettison my bag of wet swim gear by the front door as I slip inside. The kitchen is toasty warm and smells like freshly baked bread. Ryan is sitting at the table, bent over a worksheet for school as I cross to the fridge and help myself to a can of Pepsi.

"Where's Vince?" my brother asks.

I crack the tab on the aluminum can and empty its contents into a glass from the dishwasher, all while watching the trio of dark figures in the distance. The tallest one, Vince, is fading to a shadow on the ground as darkness continues its unassailable conquest of the yard.

"He's talking to his uncle. Do you need help with your homework?" I ask, sliding into Vince's usual seat.

"That's okay. It's only geography." Ryan picks up an orange pencil and begins colouring another province on his map of Canada.

A few minutes later, the front door opens to admit dad and Vince. Vince and I share a look as dad hangs up his plaid jacket and hat, although the smile that follows that look carries a strange weight, like Vince is silently begging me to play along—to maintain the façade for as long as possible.

So I say, "I can never remember which province is to the left of Ontario. Is it Manitoba or Saskatchewan?"

A flicker of relief ignites in Vince's eyes. They dart sideways in mock recollection. "I'm not sure. Manitoba, I think."

"British Columbia, Alberta, Saskatchewan, Manitoba, Ontario, and Quebec," Ryan rattles off proudly. "I know all the Maritime provinces, the territories, and the Great Lakes, too."

"That's great," Vince enthuses. Slowly, he's returning to his typical, composed self. He drapes his jacket on one of the pegs and removes his shoes before approaching the table and checking Ryan's progress over my shoulder. "Looks like you don't need my help at all tonight."

"Nope," Ryan quips. He sets to work on another one of the prairie provinces, smothering Saskatchewan in buttercup yellow.

By the time I look up from the page, Vince is halfway up the stairs. I trail after him, leaving my Pepsi on the table in case Ryan wants to finish it. When I arrive in the attic, Vince is pacing in front of his bed, shaking his head as if trapped in a losing argument with himself.

"Vince?"

The agitated behaviour ceases at the sound of my voice. He stills his hands, which are making a mess of his hair, and clears his throat in embarrassment.

"Are you okay?" I ask.

His recovery is flawless. "Of course I am."

"So, what was that all about? Out there." I indicate the window, where Rick's truck is pulling out onto the road, chased by a plume of choking black smoke.

It takes Vince a minute to find the words. In that time, the tension drains from his face and he combs his hair down with his fingers, summoning the impression that his restless state was nothing more than an illusion.

"My mother is prone to excessive worrying," he says, "so much that I moved out. The plan was to live with my uncle, but he said I'd stand to gain more from coming here." Vince pauses to let the words sink in. "She's not used to me living on my own yet. She doesn't believe I can comfortably handle the stress."

This makes perfect sense to me. It won't be long before I have to leave the nest, and mom will undoubtedly make herself sick with worry. Even in the age of cell phones and Internet, it's no substitute for actually being there if something goes wrong.

"I apologize if my behaviour caused you or your father any distress. My outburst was unprofessional, to say the least."

"That's okay. Like you said, we all have bad days."

All at once, the regular evening commotion rises up through the house. Mom bustles around the kitchen, trying to recruit Ryan into setting the table, or at least making enough room for some plates and a basket of dinner rolls. One floor up, dad walks from his study to the bathroom for a shower. His whistling is loud and clear, and seems especially pronounced as he passes beneath the attic. The warbling note echoes through the floorboards, reminding us that he's watching everything we do.

"Gabby?" dad calls up the stairs. "Could you give your mother a hand, please?"

Maybe it's not such a bad thing, living with your parents. At least you always have some excuse to escape an uncomfortable conversation.

"Okay!" I call back, hoping Vince doesn't hear the relief in my voice.

He gazes down at his bed, as if debating whether 6:00 is too early to go to sleep. I'm halfway down the steps when he says, "Gabby?"

I freeze, clutching the railing. Vince inches closer to the opening, but his desire to speak is extinguished by mom and Ryan's squabbling. I trot down the last few steps, leaving Vince, once again, out in the cold.

Chapter 10

I'm so compelled to talk to Vince about his behaviour that I wake up thirty minutes earlier the next morning. His bed is made and the coffee set to brew by the time I've changed into a pair of jeans and tamed the tangle of curls springing away from my head. I tiptoe past Ryan's room: his bed is a knot of sheets and scrawny limbs pointing in every direction. I reach for the brass knob and pull the door closed.

I pour some coffee into a travel mug and go out to meet the brisk morning. Vince's figure moves beyond the big, sliding barn door, so I quicken my steps until I'm safely out of the elements.

"Thought I'd find you here," I say as Vince saws through the baling twine with a pocketknife. I hold out the mug to him. "I brought you some coffee."

He smiles and closes the knife, tucking it into his pocket. "Thanks." Vince takes the coffee from my hands and pulls in a deep sip. After a moment, he sets the drink on the floor next to the storage room and says, "You're up early."

"I know. I was kind of hoping we could talk about last night."

His enthusiasm fades. As he bends down to gather up a generous handful of hay, he replies, "Haven't we talked enough about that already?"

"Maybe. Maybe not." I twist some hair around my finger. "I get the feeling there's something going on here, something we haven't uncovered."

Vince fidgets, avoiding my gaze. "I don't know what you're talking about."

"You asked me if I loved Jayden—and I did. But that's all changed now. *I've* changed. And you…"

Vince scatters the feed in front of the cows. Their shiny black noses plunge into the mountains of timothy hay, and soon all I can hear is their robust, mechanical chewing. "What about me?" He spreads the forage with his hands, ensuring every cow gets her own serving.

"And you… make me want to be better," I finish.

"After how I acted in my uncle's presence last night, I'm convinced anyone would aspire to more respectable conduct."

"You were annoyed. That's all."

His face relaxes. The remaining hay is doled out, and another bale retrieved, littering the floor with bits of dried grass.

Once that's done, I follow Vince to the storage room, where he rifles through the clutter to find the metal feed scoop. "I don't like it when people worry about me," he admits.

"Why not?"

"Because it makes me feel like a problem they need to solve. A burden." He hands me the tool and digs for something else.

"You don't feel like people care, when they worry about you?" If worry makes him feel like a burden, I can only imagine with love will do. Destroy his will to live, probably.

"Caring and worrying are different things. One is selfless, the other is an assumption." Vince braces his arms on the sides of the storage container where we keep our loose feed, like corn and soy beans. He directs a glance over his shoulder at me, gauging my reaction. "How does it make you feel when Tanya worries?"

I bite my lip, mostly to disguise the fact that I'm shivering. "I'm used to it."

"Then you have a lot more patience than I do."

Vince holds out his hand to accept the scoop. My fingers are stiff with cold; I should have brought mittens. I put my hands in my pockets and pretend he won't notice the bluish tint of my fingernails.

He does, naturally.

"Are you cold?" Vince asks.

"It's not that bad. I'll live."

"You're shaking." Vince pulls off his work gloves and passes them to me.

"No, thanks."

"Please take them—I've got a spare pair. At least you didn't come out here with wet hair, because I don't know how to treat hypothermia."

The insides of the gloves are toasty as I slip them on and wiggle my fingers for fit. "I'll give them back after school."

"Keep them. They're a little snug for me as it is." He exits the storage room and strides down the aisle, eager to get back to work. "I'm sorry. I don't really have time for idle talk."

"It's fine."

"You have a good day at school, all right?" he says, seizing the broom along the way. "I want to hear all about it tonight."

The rest of my family is awake when I get back to the house. Ryan is still wearing his race car pajamas, his feet thumping against the legs of the kitchen chair.

He pours milk over his cereal and eyes me suspiciously. "Where were *you?*"

"Outside." I reach for an orange from the fruit bowl.

"Kissing your boyfriend?"

"He's not my boyfriend. And we weren't kissing, we were talking." I peel off the porous rind and carefully separate the segments.

"And how's Mr. McCarthy doing today?" dad asks as he enters the room.

You mean Professor McCarthy, I think. "He's good."

"Do you like kissing him?" Ryan taunts. "Is it fun?"

With dad distracted by his quest for caffeine, I shoot Ryan a look that would get me grounded in a heartbeat. He responds by sticking out his tongue, only for it to disappear a second later. By the time dad turns away from the counter, we've practically achieved world peace.

I check the clock. The bus will be here soon. "I've got to go," I say to dad.

"Sure," he replies. "Don't forget about your swim meet tonight."

"I won't."

In the attic, I assemble my outfit for the day on my bed: powder blue jeans, a lilac t-shirt, and a white sweater that mom calls "impractical" for wearing around the barn. Through the window, I see Vince's figure drift toward the driveshed and disappear under the overhang. It's supposed to get icy tonight: dad will want him to clear the driveway and salt the veranda, but it feels like he has more on his mind today than just our safety.

When I step outside, the sun is beaming off the snow. Through the flashes of pink and green that dot my vision, I make out Vince in one of the pastures, but he has his back to me and his full attention on dad, as if it will make up for last night.

The bus screeches to a stop and I clamber up the steps as our driver utters a gruff "morning." I squeeze down the narrow aisle toward the back, but to my surprise, Trisha isn't there. I plunk down in our usual seat, and as soon as the bus lurches away from my house, I whip out my phone and shoot her a message.

Why aren't you on the bus?

We stop at Rick's farm to pick up Mike and Joel, his youngest kids. They slide into the two front seats as we roll forward again, on to the next driveway.

Trisha replies: *Emerson caught a cold at preschool and brought it home to me.*

That sucks.

Can you pick up my homework? And tell Mr. Berkley I said hi?

I agree to pick up her homework, but hold off on getting too chummy with my physics teacher. As the bus gets closer to school, I dredge up my class notes from the bottom of my backpack and review the key concepts in case Mr. Berkley decides to surprise us with another pop quiz. The inky blue heart catches my eye as I turn the page. I run my finger over its rough shape and smile, then return to the formulas with newfound appreciation.

A little while later, the bus swings into the school parking lot and the other kids spill out onto the pavement. My physics class is on the second floor, between the chemistry lab and the storage room where the biology teachers keep their life-sized models of the human skeleton. Mr. Berkley is writing some formulas on the board when I arrive. A few other people are scattered throughout the room, catching up on a backlog of studying.

Mr. Berkley hands me a piece of paper as I stride through the doorway. It's my most recent test, which flaunts a perfect score. I knew Vince's notes had the power to demystify physics, but this is too good to be true.

"Impressive, Gabby," he says. "Clearly, you've sought help with your studies."

I fold up the test. "I have this friend who's pretty good at math. He offered to give me a few pointers." I add, "By the way, Trisha is home sick today. I promised I'd pick up her homework and stuff." My gaze latches on to the stack of marked tests. Mr. Berkley hesitates momentarily, then thumbs through the pile in search of Trisha's paper. He folds it up and hands it to me, trying to be discreet, as if my best friend and I don't already tell each other everything.

"Tonight's homework is on the board," he tells me, gesturing to the white board with his marker. "A couple pages of reading and the questions on page 64. Please tell Trisha I hope she feels better soon."

"I will." More people are filing in now, so I stick both tests in my bag and take my seat.

The class drags on. By the time the bell rings, I'm itching to leave so I can drop by Trisha's other classes and collect her assignments. I have swim practice tonight, but I don't imagine Vince will object to making a house call to help a friend in need. Maybe he'll even take it as an opportunity to tell me what's truly bothering him…

Trisha's teachers seem surprised to see me, but none of them question her absence. By the time I've made my rounds, my backpack sags with the extra weight. I tuck her homework into one of my binders, sneak a glimpse at her physics mark, and head toward my next class: English.

I'm still struggling to understand *Macbeth*. My paper is starving for more than a few quotes, but every time I sit down to write, I think about Jayden, Vince, the swimming competition, and how mom and dad never should have bought the farm. Ultimately, *Macbeth* is about a guy tortured by ambition and self-doubt. I guess I could write about that, being both ambitious and wracked with self-doubt about my swimming career. But I'm not sure I'd contemplate murdering anyone for first place.

"Who is Macbeth?" my teacher, Ms. Ibarra, asks. She sweeps up and down the aisles in search of an answer. Her glasses match her violet sweater and her skirt rustles as she walks. "Any guesses?"

"The main character," Grant, at the back of the room, says. Giggles erupt from the silence.

Ms. Ibarra replies, "Well, yes, he is the title character. But who *is* he? Is he a valiant warrior, or a cold-blooded killer? What makes him *a hero*?" Her roving gaze finds a home on my face. "What do you think, Gabby? Imagine you're Macbeth and you've just killed King Duncan to secure the throne. Would this be a moment of celebration or a moment of reconciliation?"

I blink a few times, trying to clear my thoughts. The air thickens with anticipation, and I can see Grant unwrapping a Cheshire Cat smile just for me.

"I don't know," I say softly. More giggles.

Ms. Ibarra's expression softens. "Let's ignore Macbeth for a sec. Imagine, if you will, doing something that is objectively bad for reasons that are objectively good. What would be running through your mind in the aftermath of the crime?"

My mind flashes on Jayden: his pink-tinged eyes, his soft, full lips never meeting my mouth again. What was running through my mind that night? I can't say the real answer out loud, so I settle for a half-truth instead.

"I'd be thinking that the bad thing was worth the risk of being happy."

Ms. Ibarra raises her brows and resumes her slow march back to the front of the room.

"Let's talk about supporting characters," she says, wiping the board clean. And I don't hear another word she says for the rest of the class.

I make a run for the truck as an icy rain pummels my face. If Tanya was being tough on me before, she's absolutely ruthless now. On the flip side, I finally broke thirty-five seconds in the 50-meter freestyle.

"You've got speed and technique," she said as I dragged myself, breathless and burning with exertion, out of the water. "Now all you need is a winning attitude, and you're set to smoke the competition."

"Oh, there will be smoke," I promised. "My lungs are on fire."

Tanya patted my back and walked away with her head held high, while I limped back to the changeroom.

Vince has the heat cranked to high when I climb into the passenger seat beside him.

"How'd it go?" He's decided not to accompany me into the rec centre anymore, so I can "focus on my ambitions." Little does he know he's always present in my mind, cheering me on every stroke.

I bust out a grin. "I broke thirty-five seconds."

"You're amazing." Vince puts the truck in gear. "Home now?"

"Not yet. I need to drop off Trisha's homework."

"Where does she live?"

"In the fancy part of town. Her parents are doctors." Vince drives toward the road, checks both ways, and hangs a left. I stare at his hands on the wheel and wonder if there's anything they can't do.

I direct him to Mapleview Court, a winding stretch of manicured lawns and attached garages where Trisha lives with her mom, dad, older sister, and three-year-old nephew. Trisha's family moved to Canada when she was seven so her dad could open his own practice, and she's been looking for ways to escape this icy hellscape ever since.

"It's the big grey one, number 1782," I tell Vince, pointing to the driveway. He pulls up to the black garage door as I pull the binder full of notes out of my backpack. I stuff the pages into my coat to protect them from the sleet, zip it up, and dash toward the front door.

The doorbell clangs. A few moments later, Trisha comes to the door and sniffles loudly.

"Hey," I say, "how are you feeling?"

"Like an elephant is sitting on my face." Trisha stifles a cough. "Did you bring my homework?"

As she steps aside to let me enter the foyer, I unzip my coat and pass her the slightly-crumpled stack of assignments. "Also, Mr. Berkley says he hopes you feel better soon."

"Thanks." Trisha tosses the pages onto the nearby credenza. Somewhere upstairs, Emerson lets out a cry as she says, "It's getting crazy out there, eh?"

"Yeah. I should be getting home."

"Did your dad drive you?"

"No, Vince did."

She brightens at this, then raises her hand to cover another cough. "Give him a kiss for me."

"You're gross. Go back to bed."

Trisha hovers in the doorway as I beat a hasty retreat back to the truck. The rain has almost stopped, but beneath my shoes, I can feel the driveway transforming into a skating rink. I skid the last few feet to the door, yank it open, and duck inside.

Vince raises his hand to wave at Trisha as the door closes behind her. "How is she?"

"Miserable. We should get home before all of this rain freezes."

"Agreed."

He's a careful driver. When we get to the farm, all the lights are on at the house. The trees are glazed with ice, the fence boards are dripping with icicles, and even the windchimes dazzle like diamonds as the wind struggles to hold a tune. Vince maneuvers the truck into the driveshed and turns off the engine, then reaches into the backseat to retrieve my swim gear from the floor.

"Do you really think I'm amazing?" I ask.

"Of course. Don't you?"

"I guess." I stare at the vents on the dashboard, yearning for more of their warmth.

Vince rests my bag in his lap and his gaze on my face. "Come on, Gabby. You should know by now I never say things I don't mean."

"That's true. And for the record, you're pretty amazing yourself."

"Thank you."

"No, I mean it. You can do so much."

His lips curl. I can't be sure, with the shed being so dark, but I think he's even blushing a little.

"Do you want to go inside?" he asks. "I wouldn't want your parents to misconstrue the delay in our arrival."

"What? You mean you don't want them to think we're making out?"

This time, his face practically glows. "That's a possibility," he replies, and I can't tell if he means the making out part or the one where my parents fear for my innocence.

Before I can ask for clarification, Vince pushes open the driver's door and steps outside. I know that as soon as we set foot in the house, he'll go straight to work helping mom and the spell hanging over us will be shattered, so I linger for a couple seconds in the truck, soaking up the leftover warmth and whatever possibilities he alluded to.

When I join him outside, Vince says, "Is everything okay?"

"Yeah. Perfect."

"What's wrong?"

"I don't know. A little bit of everything, I guess." My backpack still feels too heavy, even without Trisha's homework weighing me down. "Sometimes I wish I could fast forward through everything. Skip over school and training and get to the part where it all pays off."

"I know, but you wouldn't learn anything that way."

"I'd be happy though."

"But what if the joy is in the process, not the result? Why do anything if you don't enjoy it?"

I spin around, retort at the ready. He's so predictable. So clichéd. And I already know I'm going to hate the result when my feet skate over a patch of ice and my backpack heaves toward the ground.

Vince's reaction is lightning-quick: first, he drops my swim bag, then his hands close on my arms, catching me mid-fall.

"Are you okay?" he asks.

I nod, casting my eyes toward the cloudy grey ice underfoot. Vince's hands are still clutching my arms, his eyes trained intently on mine.

"I'm fine," I whisper.

Vince smiles. It's not lost on me that his hands are still holding me steady. "Good."

As he starts to let go, I say, "I think—"

He waits. "What?"

I think my heart is beating too rapidly. My fingers are still gripping his coat sleeves and I'm halfway to letting go when suddenly my mouth opens and I hear myself say, "I think I'm falling in love with you."

His eyes widen, sparking up the darkness. I stare at his lips, bracing myself for a well-rehearsed speech about the moral implications of dating his employer's daughter. Objectively, I know this is wrong: I shouldn't love Vince McCarthy for any reason, not even if that reason is because he's amazing. He's just the hired hand.

Vince pulls me to him, turns his head a little, and presses his mouth ever so gently against mine. This kiss is perfect, like everything else he does. And suddenly I don't want to fast-forward through anything. I want to stay this way forever, frozen in time between Vince's arms.

He removes his lips from mine and whispers, "So am I."

I reach for his hand and lead him toward the house. Our feet hit the bottom step in unison and he lets go of my hand, before the light from the kitchen fully settles on his face. "For now," he says. "Just until…"

I interrupt him with a firm nod of understanding. "We don't have to tell anyone if you don't want to."

"I like working here," Vince admits, "and your parents trust me. I certainly don't want to give you the impression that I'm ashamed to be seen with you, because I'm not and would never be. And to tell you the truth—"

I crack a grin at his rambling, roll forward onto my tiptoes, and kiss him again so he'll finally shut up.

Chapter 11

As winter sets in, Vince and I spend most of our time helping dad to care for our pregnant cows. The work is endless, exhausting, and wreaks so much havoc on our bodies that we collapse into bed without even saying goodnight. I can't help but think mom orchestrated this herself—that she spied us from the kitchen window the night of our first kiss and devised a plan for ensuring that no other parts of our body come anywhere near each other. In other words, the secret's out.

It's still dark when my alarm goes off. At first, I have no idea what day of the week it is, since I've been dragging myself out of bed before the sunrise for the past three months. As my mind clears, I flick my eyes at the wall and murmur, "Good morning."

"Morning," Vince replies, his voice deep and jagged. "How'd you sleep?"

"Like a baby. How's your back?"

He makes a soft groaning noise that is quickly silenced by the squeaking of the mattress. I wonder if he's facing toward me or away. "I can still work, but it won't be at my usual blistering speed."

"Good. That means I might actually be able to keep up with you." My body curls, trying to hold on to the warmth of the heavy quilt. The only thing that could possibly make my bed a more heavenly place right now is if Vince was sharing it with me, but that would only result in mom taking more drastic measures to curb our closeness. I nestle deeper under the covers, even as I hear Vince's feet hit the floor.

He materializes from behind the wall. His hair has grown since he came to live with us, and it's so adorably unkempt that a smile breaks over my face before I can stop it.

"You know, I'm starting to realize that I don't know anything about you," I say, tucking the blanket under my chin.

Vince quirks a brow. He's not wearing his glasses yet, so I can only imagine I must look like a giant burrito from his vantage point. "What do you mean?"

"I mean, you've been living with us since September and I don't even know the names of your siblings." This suddenly seems like a significant obstacle in our relationship. If you want to truly understand who someone is, you have to start with where they came from, and no one who has siblings emerges from the past unscathed. "Isn't that kind of weird?"

"Not that I have any desire to start an argument with you at five-thirty in the morning, but you've never shown much interest in knowing anything about my family."

"I'm interested now."

Vince smirks, but to my vast and crushing disappointment, doesn't come to sit beside me.

"I'm the oldest, as I've said before. Then there's Natalie. She's only a couple months younger than you. Lillian is fourteen. Emily is eleven, Chloe and Olivia are both nine, and Adam is seven. Natalie, Lillian, and I share the same father, although, between us," Vince pauses to shrug, "I think dad liked Natalie the best."

"Hard to imagine anyone can compete with *you*." If Vince is perfect, then I don't think there's a word for what Natalie is.

"Not really. As I've said, I have my flaws." He pushes away from the wall and faces the stairs. "See you downstairs?"

"Yeah, I'll be right there."

After he leaves, I lie around some more, trying to envision a slightly younger, female version of Vince. I'll bet she's blonde and fit and witty and reads the dictionary for fun. Even if she doesn't end up curing cancer or saving the environment, she'll still be lightyears ahead of me, blessed by the kind of ambition that Tanya and my parents wish I possessed.

I finally manage to get dressed, brush my teeth, and wrangle my hair under one of dad's toques. When I get down to the kitchen, I see that Vince has decided to skip breakfast, so I take his lead and head out into the bitingly cold air. So much for setting a pace I can keep up with. My jacket rustles with each step and my boots carve deep wells into the snow, breaking through the thin layer of ice with a satisfying crunch. Maybe dad will let me drive the tractor this morning, so Vince doesn't have all the fun.

I slip inside the old wooden structure to find them both huddled near the milking machines. Vince is crouched on the floor next to one of the cows, and dad is towering over him, directing Vince's hands and showing him where to attach the various components.

As I walk toward them, dad looks at me and says, "You want to get started on the driveway?"

"You mean I can drive the tractor?" Excitement knocks my heart against my ribs. "By myself?"

"Yes, as long as you go slowly." Reaching into the pocket of his coat, dad produces the keys and drops them into my eagerly cupped palms.

"Start down by the house and leave a path for your mother to get out with her car," he instructs, "then circle back and start clearing the area around the pastures. And remember what I told you about slopes: go slowly and steer downhill, not uphill, so you don't tip over."

The sky is turning a dusty rose colour by the time I reach the tractor and climb into the cold, plastic seat. I fasten the seatbelt around my waist and stick the key into the ignition. As the engine awakens with a chilly growl, I slide the ear muffs over my head and scan the grey wasteland for potential hazards. After babysitting Ryan, this is the most responsibility I've had since we moved here. I bask in my button-bursting pride for a second or two, then lower the pusher and drive through the snow, watching it crest in noisy, white waves all the way down the driveway.

I spend most of the morning this way, going up and down the driveway as if it were a swimming pool. The tractor lurches over every rut and gash in the ground that isn't filled with snow, and soon my backside feels like it used to after a whole day of tobogganing as a kid.

Vince approaches me as I'm rounding the side of the barn. His mouth opens, but I don't catch a word he says until I stop moving.

"What?" I ask.

He scales the side of the mighty green beast and lifts one of my ear muffs. "I said, you're doing great."

"Oh. Thanks."

Vince drops to the ground and disappears into the barn. It's only been a few hours since we started working, but I'm already exhausted. My fingers wrap around the wheel again and I cut a beeline back to the shed, leaving the yard as clean as the pages in Vince's sketchbook.

Once all the equipment is shut off and put away, I return to the barn to see the cows are in the middle of being milked and Vince is sweeping the aisles. I could get used to this routine: being useful, watching Vince work, while dad whistles like a songbird somewhere nearby. I try to ignore the reality that Vince won't be with us forever, at least while I'm still riding the high of my newfound independence.

"I'm starting to think we make a pretty good team," I tell him, sliding my hands into my coat pockets.

Vince raises his eyes to mine and smiles. "We do."

The barn settles into a noisy kind of silence. It must be almost lunchtime, because my stomach makes an obnoxious whining noise that sets my face on fire.

"Hungry?" Vince asks.

"I said I could keep up with you, and I will." I motion for him to surrender the broom, and he leaves to find another one while I swish the remaining scraps of debris out the door and onto my freshly plowed masterpiece.

"So, I've been thinking." Vince's voice behind me prompts me to turn around. "Would you like to meet my family?"

All these months, I've been wondering what Vince and I are to each other. I know we're roommates, and most people would call us friends, but I knew he was worth holding on to long before he saved me from breaking my neck on that patch of ice. And I know I didn't break up with Jayden for nothing, or I wouldn't be saying what I'm about to say now.

"I'd love to. Especially Natalie, if she's as amazing as you are."

"Okay."

"Okay?"

Vince cups his hands around my face. His gloves are scratchy against my skin, but so warm that I feel like melting. He kisses me softly, then turns and walks down the aisle as if I dreamed the whole thing. And maybe I am dreaming when, less than a minute later, he falls to the floor and starts seizing uncontrollably.

"Vince?" I wait, but I don't wake up. And Vince is still lying on the floor, his limbs jerking and his eyes rolled back in his head. I scream dad's name, because it's clear Vince can't hear me and I don't know what to do. All that confidence I gained from driving the tractor is gone.

The muscles in his hands contract, clenching his fingers into fists. Dad comes running over to us as the convulsions work their way down to Vince's hips and knees. A trickle of saliva gathers at the corner of his mouth and spills onto the floor.

Dad puts his hands on my shoulders and moves me aside so he can kneel beside Vince.

"When did this start?" dad asks me.

"I don't know. A few seconds ago."

Dad unzips Vince's coat and loosens the clothing around his throat. Vince chokes out more noises and saliva. I want to stop all this, to end his suffering, but when I try to intervene, dad lays a hand on my arm.

"It's okay. It should be over in a minute or two." Sure enough, as he says this, the jerking motions ebb until they are nothing more than gentle aftershocks. Dad turns Vince on his side and speaks in a soothing voice. "That's it. You're okay. We're right here." He rubs Vince's arm until he slowly regains consciousness.

Dazed, Vince opens his eyes and coughs a couple of times. He's still shaking as dad guides him into an upright position. I don't think the barn has ever been this quiet.

Dad is surprisingly calm about the ordeal. He brushes the dirt from Vince's back like he's done it a million times, then says, "How's your head? I think Gabby saw you go down, but she couldn't get to you in time."

Vince looks up at me, but I don't speak. He caught me that night, and I just let him fall. What kind of friend does that make me?

Dad helps Vince to his feet. "Come on. I'm going to take you to the hospital so we can get your head checked out."

"I'll come, too," I say.

"Gabby, I think it's best if you stay here. Tell your mother I'll call as soon as I can."

Dad and Vince head out to the truck. The engine starts up with a grating roar, and as they back away from the barn, I catch sight of the disappointment in Vince's gaze.

It turns out I was right about what I said in the attic this morning: I don't know Vince McCarthy at all.

Chapter 12

Hours pass, but dad doesn't call. He and Vince have been gone for so long, I'm starting to think they went back to Vince's hometown. Now I see why his mom was so worried. And Rick—he must've already known what Vince was dealing with. That's why he dumped him here, why he felt the need to drop in unannounced. All those nights Vince drove me to the pool could've put us both in the hospital. What's going to happen when mom and dad realize he can no longer operate the tractor? I know the answer, but I can't bring myself to look it in the eyes. It hovers in my periphery like Tanya's figure at the end of the pool, reminding me with every breath that I'm in for a world of pain.

Finally, at around eight o'clock, a pickup truck with muddy yellow headlights turns into our driveway. As it lumbers toward the house, I bolt from my desk and run downstairs. Mom has already fed Ryan and sent him to his room to do homework, so I know she's expecting some kind of family feud. I don't care though, because Vince is home. Whatever happens next, we'll get through it together—assuming dad lets him stay.

I reach for the front door and yank it open. The air outside hits me like a gut-punch, stealing my breath. Dad parks directly in front of the house and turns off the engine, letting the two rectangular beams of light fade to dull brown blotches. After an excruciating delay, the passenger door opens and Vince unfurls from the truck's warmth. It's too dark to see his face, but his shoulders are hunched and his head is bowed. I bite my lip at the sight of his unsteady gait. Did they prescribe him something for pain, or is this the ghost of today's seizure? I cram my feet into a pair of boots and dash outside, ready to catch him if he falls.

As his foot meets the bottom step, I wrap my arms around his shoulders and breathe in the antiseptic aroma clinging to his hair and clothes. Vince lets out an involuntary grunt of pain, forcing me to withdraw.

"Are you okay?" I ask as I look him over.

His mouth barely moves when he replies, "Just a bit sore."

I release my gentle but protective hold on his arms. Vince climbs the steps and enters the kitchen behind me, issuing a brief greeting to mom before dragging himself upstairs. Dad isn't far behind, and one look at his grizzled face tells me everything I need to know, and more. Since Vince wasn't as forthcoming with his affections, I wrap my arms around dad's familiar-smelling plaid jacket and hold him tightly.

Dad encloses me with his left hand. His right one holds a collection of pamphlets with shiny covers and purple ribbons printed on the front. More homework.

"What did the doctor say?" I ask.

Dad ushers me into the house, saying, "I don't know. I spent most of the day in waiting rooms."

He places the brochures in my hand. We step into the kitchen and dad closes the door behind us. As he hangs up his jacket and hat, I fan the pamphlets out across the table. I've never known anyone with epilepsy, and now I'm about to become an expert in this terrible, debilitating disorder.

Mom reaches for one of the leaflets. I don't think I've ever seen her this pale. "How did we not know?" she asks dad.

"He didn't tell us." Even though it's late, dad goes straight for the coffee pot and pours himself whatever's left of the oily black substance. "Gabby, why don't you go check on Vince and make sure he's okay?"

I nod, leaving the brochures on the table. I can only hope Ryan's already asleep, so he'll be spared the worst of mom and dad's squabble over Vince's future with us, which was tenuous at best. Now, it may be nonexistent.

When I reach the attic, Vince is sifting through his clothes. His back is facing me, and his jeans are streaked with dirt from the barn floor. If I didn't know better, I'd think he just got in from nighttime chores instead of a whole day of talking to doctors.

Vince stands up and turns toward the stairs, startling a little when he sees me. His grip tightens on the bundle of clean clothes as I step toward him and brush back the hair from his scar. His skin is warm beneath my touch. I think of the brochures downstairs, with their violet ribbons and blocky letters, trying to convey what I already know: that people like Vince are more than their disability, and no amount of dark days will overshadow what I feel for him.

"I have epilepsy," he says.

"I know." I drop my hand. "You could've told me."

"If I actually believed that, I would've."

"You don't think I could've handled the truth?"

"No. I'm saying *I* couldn't handle it." Vince lets out a breath. "I couldn't handle the thought of losing what we had. I know how selfish that sounds, but every time I get close to someone, I get scared. I worry about what's going to happen if I can't control my seizures."

In my mind, I replay Vince's seizure like a bad dream, hunting for meaning in every detail. The pale slits of his eyes. The tense set of his hands. The guttural moans. If that's what control looks like, I'm afraid to consider the alternative.

"How long has this been going on?" I ask.

"Since I was a baby. I had my first seizure when I was only a few months old, and after that they became a regular occurrence. My childhood was a patchwork of doctor's appointments, hospital visits, and tutors, since I missed a lot of school. Making friends was difficult, as you can imagine." He gestures toward the window. "I wanted to come out here because I thought it would be good for me. I hadn't had a seizure in a couple of years and I wanted to experience life on a working farm. I wasn't expecting to meet you, Gabby. Maybe if I had, I wouldn't have come, so I wouldn't have to put you through this."

I'm about to tell him that his epilepsy won't change anything between us when he steps around me and descends the stairs. And, just like that, we're back at square one, with one of us pushing and the other pulling away.

Vince has gone to take a shower, so I sulk back to the kitchen feeling restless and itchy with stress. The brochures are still on the table, and dad is sitting across from them with glassy, bloodshot eyes. His catatonic state traps me in the doorway.

Mom, whose back is facing me, says, "You know he can't stay here."

Dad bobs his head in agreement.

"It's too risky. What if it happens when he's driving the tractor?" mom goes on.

"I know." Dad rests his elbows on the table. "I'd hate to ask him to leave, but if he can't—" He raises his gaze to mine. "How long have you been standing there?"

"About ten seconds." I can't tell if this is a long time, but judging by the context, I have to assume it's an eternity. Since we're on the topic of Vince, I say, "Vince seems to be feeling better. He's in the shower right now."

"That's good. Now, why don't you go upstairs and work on your essay so your mother and I can talk?"

Rather than complying with this simple request, I trek toward the sink and fill a glass with water, sipping it slowly in front of the window. Dad should know by now that I'm not a child, or there would have been no need for him to install a wall in the middle of my room.

"You can drink water upstairs," dad says when I've drained half the glass. "It's late, and your mother and I—"

"Need to talk. I know." I turn away from the sink. "I'm not ten years old. I know what's going on here."

"This is not a discussion for you to be involved in," he intones.

"Oh, it's not? Last I checked, I was still a part of this family. And this definitely seems like a family matter." Dad sighs. "Vince is my friend. And you're not going to send him away."

"Gabby, I don't think you realize how serious this situation is."

"I do. I was *there*."

Mom chimes in, "Then you'll understand why we're concerned. The reality is, Vince lied. He should've told us about the seizures months ago, and he should not have been driving you or Ryan anywhere."

"So, what? You think he's proud of this? That's not Vince, mom. He feels like shit right now."

"Language," dad murmurs.

I snatch the brochures up. "Look, no one would've made these if they weren't important. So let's read them. For Vince. We can make it safe for him here."

"Gabby, we can't," mom insists, closing her eyes. "Please try to understand this—"

"Understand what, exactly? That because he has a disability, he should be treated differently? When you thought I had ADHD, you were prepared to turn our lives upside down to make mine easier. But I guess the same measures don't apply to Vince, because he's just the hired help. Right?"

"We never said that."

"You didn't need to. The truth is like Vince's seizures: it comes out whether you want it to or not."

I hover next to the sink, clutching the fistful of pamphlets. Mom and dad say nothing, as I predicted. Whatever. I'll deal with this on my own.

By the time I get to the attic, Vince's half of the room is dark. There's enough residual light from the second floor hallway to illuminate the outline of his body beneath the covers. I lean forward slightly and whisper, "Vince?"

He doesn't stir. I creep closer to the futon, but he's buried in the bed's warmth. After the day he's had, I can't blame him for wanting to disappear for a while.

I leave Vince to his rest and walk around the wall to my side of the room. I set the brochures on my desk and open my laptop, but my

English essay is the farthest thing from my mind in this moment. Even if I'm the only one who cares about Vince's wellbeing, I'm determined to care with every inch. When I dive into a pool, I dive deep. It's the only way to get ahead.

Hours pass. I read everything I can, beginning with the brochures, until I hear the door to mom and dad's bedroom close. One website goes into detail about how to care for a person before, during, and after a seizure. Another describes the different kinds of epilepsy and how they affect the brain. Based on what I saw in the barn today, Vince is most likely suffering from tonic-clonic seizures, which produce the classic, full-body convulsions most people think of when they hear the word epilepsy.

I'm about to close my laptop when the page I'm skimming mentions sudden unexpected death. The brain controls everything—heart rate, breathing, organ function. Sometimes, if the seizures are protracted, the rest of the body suffers and eventually shuts down. For some people with epilepsy, going to bed means sleeping forever.

I picture Vince on the opposite side of the wall, fresh off a seizure none of us saw coming. If it happened once, it can happen again. And probably, it'll happen when no one's around. Then what? My mind flashes through the jumble of information. *Remain calm. Wait for it to pass. If the person does not regain consciousness, call 911.* But none of these solutions address the real issue here, which is that no one can be with him all the time. Not even if we're sleeping in the same room.

Very quietly, I slide back my chair and tiptoe around the partition. If I lean in close enough, I can hear Vince breathing in a slow tidal rhythm, the sound rising on the intake and softening as it leaves his lungs. So peaceful, not like the strangled wheezes he made this morning.

I climb into my bed, facing the wall, and think about Vince and his epilepsy until sleep overtakes me.

Chapter 13

Dad lets Vince take the next day off. The mood around the house is subdued, the conversations brief and antiseptic. Around ten o'clock, mom heads to the supermarket with Ryan, and it's so quiet in the kitchen that I can hear the fridge's motor humming. The sound is driving me insane, so I shut my laptop, pull on my boots and coat, and step outside. Even here, the silence is agonizing; the snow muffles the softer noises, making my footsteps louder than a construction site. I break a path through the drifts, targeting the spots that are glazed with ice, and the silvery swells shatter like glass under my weight.

The barn looks the same. The cows are as docile as ever, unmoved by what they witnessed yesterday. The tangy odor of the animals rushes to fill my nose as I stride down the aisle in search of something to do, but dad's been up for hours making sure our Holsteins stick to their feeding and milking schedule. After last night, I wonder if he's still planning to make Vince leave, or if doing the work of two people has made him realize how vital good help is to the success of our operation.

I approach the door that overlooks the paddocks and find dad fixing the gate. He dabs some oil on the hinges to kill the endless squeaking, and only notices me walking toward him when the sound finally abates.

"How's the essay coming?" he asks.

"Slowly." I claw some hair back from my mouth and pin it behind my ear. "I'm taking a break."

"I can see that." Dad flicks his eyes at me. "Can you give me a hand?"

I raise the gate off the ground as he tightens the screws holding it to the post. Normally this would be Vince's job, but he woke up this morning feeling like he'd been hit by a bus, and after forcing down some coffee and scrambled eggs, he crawled back up to the attic to sleep another couple of hours.

Once dad finishes with the hinge, he asks, "How's Vince?"

"Still tired. Some people recover from seizures immediately, or it can take days. I think it's called the postictal phase."

Dad turns away from the post looking surprised. "You've been reading the brochures." It's not a question per se, but all the same, I nod.

"I've read a little bit," I admit. "How did you know what to do yesterday, when Vince had his seizure?"

The gate is once again functional. Dad gives it a couple test swings and puts the WD-40 back in his tool box. "In college I had a friend who was epileptic. His seizures weren't as bad as Vince's, but I learned what I could."

"Did you ever worry…" Dad looks at me until I finish my sentence. "About him not waking up?"

He nods. "You know, a lot of people with epilepsy lead otherwise normal lives. There are medications and therapies that can help control the seizures. Even dietary changes can help."

"Does this mean Vince gets to stay?"

Dad's face crumples in thought. I hadn't expected him to arrive at a decision overnight—I mean, it took years for him and mom to go from dreaming about the farm to actually owning one—but I feel like it should be a simple choice: either Vince is a part of our family now, or he's gone like last week's leftovers.

"If you're not busy with homework, I could use some more help," dad says. He leads the way back to the barn carrying his tools in one hand and his hat in the other. "At least until Vince feels better."

Hope flushes through my veins, making my cheeks warm. I follow dad to the storage room, but I've already made up my mind: when Vince wakes up, I want him to know I'm always going to be there for him, even when the seizures try to scare me away.

"Actually, I really should get back to work. That essay won't write itself," I tell him.

"Good choice." Dad retrieves some more supplies and heads out on his next mission. His whistling starts up, ringing loud and clear through the barn, before the giant pillows of snow steal the music from the air.

*

When the last bell rings, everyone springs from their seats in a clamor of boots and backpacks. Grant and the other jocks, who were barely conscious during class, are suddenly and irritatingly restored. They perform some elaborate fist-bump routine and walk toward the door, dropping the volume of the room by about fifty percent. As I gather up my stuff, Ms. Ibarra glances up from her desk and smiles.

"How's the essay coming along?" she asks.

"I'm kind of struggling. If you have a few minutes, maybe I could show you what I have so far?"

Ms. Ibarra nods, her thin black brows raised in expectation. I dig my notes out of my bag and hand them to her, then stand there gnawing on my bottom lip while she skims each page.

Vince was awake when I returned to the house yesterday. His headache had faded, but he still felt sick with guilt, especially after I told him dad was working alone. We talked about some of the websites I'd read, and he seemed surprised that I'd taken the initiative to educate myself on his disorder, since, in Vince's words, I'm "learning averse."

"This isn't like school," I explained to him. "School is so long, and most of what we learn has no application. But this." He looked up at me then, his eyes still veiny from sleep. "This is different. Important."

"Well, it *is* different," Vince agreed in a scratchy voice that made me wonder if he'd been crying instead of sleeping. "But I'm not that important. You and your family have bigger issues to contend with, and shouldn't go out of your way to accommodate me."

"Too late. Mom already likes you and dad needs all the help he can get. Plus, if you leave now, we'll have to find Ryan a new tutor, and the last three quit inside of a week." This last part was a lie, or at least a balloon-animal version of the truth, blown up and twisted into

133

something pretty. The last three tutors were mom, dad, and myself, and we had to stop helping Ryan because none of us understood the homework either. So, despite what Vince said, I knew his role in our family was larger than anything the four of us alone could have achieved. For now, we would have to learn to live with his epilepsy, just like I learned to live with the wall in my room.

Ms. Ibarra finishes reading my rough draft and shuffles the pages into a neat stack. "Well, you're off to a strong start. I was impressed with the answer you gave in class the other day, when I asked who Macbeth was."

I stare down at my hands. "I used to think Shakespeare was a waste of time, but I guess some of his plays are still relevant to today's problems."

"He's one of the greats for a reason. So much of his work is about the pain of being human. Romeo and Juliet is about not being able to have the one you want. King Lear is about betrayal and forgiveness. Sometimes, you have to be prepared to dig deep to understand what's really going on."

"I know." Ms. Ibarra hands me back my essay as I say, "My essay may end up being longer than ten pages. Is that okay?"

"Of course, as long as you're not padding your word count. I look forward to reading the rest."

I slip the backpack's straps over my shoulders and make my way across the empty classroom toward the hall. Aside from a few stragglers who are huddled around a locker, everyone has already gone home. I have just enough time to collect the rest of my belongings before the bus leaves and I'm stuck begging mom for a ride, since calling Vince is now officially out of the question.

As I turn the corner, the click-clack of heels echoes throughout the hall. Trisha runs toward me, her bag slapping against her hip.

"Gabby," Trisha huffs, "thank god you're still here."

"Is everything okay?"

"Of course not. Would I be running in heels if everything was peachy?" She swings her bag under her arm and unearths a piece of paper, sticking it under my nose. "Berkley gave me an F. I can't take an F home to my parents."

I scan her answers in silence. Trisha took the same approach to her physics test that I did a few weeks ago, jotting down random equations and hoping one of them stuck. In the margins, Mr. Berkley wrote: *Needs work!*

"He's brutal," I say, passing the test back to her.

"I know. So, what time can I come over?"

"What? You mean, tonight?"

"No, next year." Trisha's deadpan expression flexes into a smile. "I need to speak with a certain nerdy blond."

My chest tightens. I haven't figured out how to tell Trisha about Vince's epilepsy: he's so private, I'm not sure he'd appreciate finding her nose in his business. But by keeping it a secret, I'm only reinforcing the stigma of living with a disability. Either way, I'm sure Trisha will understand, coming from a family of doctors.

"I'll call you when I get home," I say, zipping up my coat so quickly, it snags. After wresting the zipper free, I cram the rest of my books into my backpack and shut the door with a resonant clang. "Mom will want me to clean the place up a bit before you come. You know how she is."

"I thought that was Vince's job."

"It is, but I should still talk to her first."

We make our way outside to find a deserted parking lot and the last bus—ours—idling by the doors. We climb the steps and take our seats at the rear, pretending we didn't hear the driver grumbling about our tardiness. The bus lurches forward seconds before we sit down. All the way to Trisha's house, I mark her physics test while she reads my essay. When it's all said and done, she places the pages in my lap and declares, "If you don't get an A on that, I'll go on a hunger strike."

"Really? You think it's that good?"

"Gabby, it's amazing. I don't know where you learned to write like that…" When I don't offer any insight into my supposedly brilliant muse, she changes the subject. "So, you and Vince. How's that going?"

I lean my head back against the seat. The sun hangs like a pearl against the silk-blue sky, and its brightness is mirrored in the mountains of snow guarding the curbs around town. It's only been two days since Vince's seizure; two days since I discovered that you can know someone without actually knowing them at all. I never got a chance to ask Vince if he forgives me for not catching him. If it were me having the seizures, it would be enough just knowing someone cares.

"We're taking our time. We still have a lot to learn about each other," I say.

"Oh, yeah? Like what?"

Oh, I don't know. Like how to recognize when someone's about to experience a seizure. Or how to prevent them from choking on their own vomit. Or when, exactly, to call for an ambulance. "The nitty gritty stuff. You know, like how Jayden and I could read each other's minds."

"So, what you're saying is, you and Vince are endgame."

"I wouldn't go that far. But he's definitely a keeper." Or maybe I'm his. Only time will tell what the future holds for me and the boy in the attic.

*

Mom is fine with Trisha coming over, provided we get some actual studying done instead of wasting the visit on gossip. Around seven o'clock, after my family, Vince, and I have eaten dinner and cleaned up the kitchen, Trisha comes skidding down the driveway in her dad's BMW, blasting music loud enough to shake the house. I wait for her in the doorway, shivering in my loose white t-shirt and baggy jogging pants, while she unloads her stuff from the passenger seat.

"Why is your driveway so long?" she asks, as if it didn't take her a grand total of five seconds to go from the road to our house. She's got such a lead foot, I'm surprised she passed her G2 on the first attempt.

"Dad's a people-phobe." I step aside so she can enter the kitchen. "Did you want me to make popcorn? I think we still have that dill seasoning."

"Nah, that's okay. I only need a little help."

"In that case, you overpacked." I motion to her arms, stretched to their limits around a humungous pile of books.

Trisha sighs. "I always do." She drops the books on the table with a bang, making me flinch. I remember reading on one site that loud, unexpected noises can be a seizure trigger for some people with epilepsy. Thankfully, Vince is in the basement helping dad fix the furnace and probably can't hear much of anything beyond the thick, stone walls.

I decide to go ahead and make popcorn, knowing that Trisha always overstays her welcome anyway. As the bag slowly begins to inflate and our kitchen teems with its buttery scent, she plunks herself down in a chair and says, "Where is everyone?"

"Dad and Vince are downstairs doing manly stuff. Mom's helping Ryan get ready for bed."

"Now? But it's seven o'clock."

"Trust me, we're going to need that much time." I retrieve a bowl from the cupboard and set it next to the microwave.

As the popping tapers into silence, I pull out the bag and pinch the top open, releasing a cloud of steam. The kernels clink into the bowl. Once the bag is empty, I fumble around in the spices until I locate the artificially-flavoured dill pickle powder. Say what you will about processed food, but at least they've come up with a way to make popcorn even more irresistible.

As Trisha is leafing through her notes, Vince emerges from the basement. I should be accustomed to him appearing out of thin air by now, but my heart still skips at the sight of him. We share a smile that says *everything is okay* as he walks into the kitchen and over to the sink for a glass of water.

"Hey," Vince and I say in unison. I gesture to my best friend. "You remember Trisha."

"How could I forget?" Vince replies, bringing the glass to his lips.

Trisha faces him with an incandescent grin. "You couldn't, obviously. And *I* haven't forgotten that you are a whiz at physics."

As Vince eyes me uncomprehendingly, I explain, "Trisha bombed her physics test. Is it okay if I let her borrow your notes?"

"Fine by me." He drains the glass and places it in the sink. Ever since his seizure, he's been more cautious than usual. Ryan isn't allowed to keep any of his toys downstairs, but in the event that one migrates to the living room, Vince is quick to pick it up. Tables are subject to a harsh side-eye. He seems especially suspicious of the boot rack, which is ordinarily a disaster, although I've been making an effort to keep it tidy. It's not much, but if it helps him feel safe, it's worth the extra trouble.

As he turns to leave, I tell Trisha, "The binder's in my room. I'll run up and get it."

"Cool. Oh, and can you bring your laptop? I need to Google a few things."

I head upstairs to retrieve the necessary supplies. I've disconnected my computer from its charging cable when Trisha screams my name, and I know exactly why.

Vince is having another seizure.

I race downstairs. My mind is clearer this time, less confused about how to respond. Like when I dive into a pool and my limbs automatically propel me forward, back to the surface for air. Sure enough, as I reach the bottom step, I see Vince lying on the living room floor, his body overcome with spasms. His head is tipped back slightly, and though his eyes are looking in my direction, I know he can't see me at all. The horrible choking noise I've come to associate with Vince's seizures fills the room.

"It's okay," I say as I take my place at his side, "I'm here, Vince." I remove his glasses, fold them, and set them on the coffee table for safekeeping. He's wearing a loose shirt, so we're good on that front. Now, all that's left to do is wait.

Trisha lowers her hands from her mouth. Her eyes are wide and her cheeks are a sickly colour I've never seen before. "Should we put a pencil in his mouth?"

"No, that's a myth. If we put anything in his mouth, he's bound to choke on it." I glance at the clock on the wall, adding, "He's not in control of his body right now."

Trisha stands board-stiff in my periphery, watching the seizure run its course. Her gawking infuriates me. Vince's epilepsy isn't a spectacle or some trendy disease inspiring an online aesthetic. It's torture—for him, for us, for the people working to find a cure. No one wants an audience in their most vulnerable moments.

So I say, "Could you get my sweater? It's hanging on the back of my chair in the kitchen." This yields no reaction, so I bark, "Now, Trish!"

She scurries from the room. A moment later, she sheepishly hands me my sweater, which I roll up and tuck under Vince's head. The saliva is starting; at least the fabric will absorb some of it.

A couple minutes after it begins, the seizure comes to an end. Vince's movements slow to a gentler rhythm. As his muscles relax, I guide him into the recovery position by lifting his knee and turning his hips, until he's lying on his front with his hand under his cheek. He's bound to be exhausted and in pain once he regains full consciousness, so I prepare myself for the reality that I'll be completing tonight's chores alone.

"That's it. It's okay—you're safe," I say. Vince blinks a few times, trying to orient himself once again. It's only when I'm massaging his arm that I notice the dark stain on his pants and Trisha nowhere to be found.

Vince is confused; he has no memory of the few seconds leading up to the seizure (basically around the time I went to fetch my laptop and his physics notes). In a way, this is a relief: maybe he'll forget Trisha was here, or that she saw him collapse and soil himself.

He's so weak, too. Getting him into an upright position is way harder than dad made it look, but I manage. I'm trying not to stare at the wet patch on his jeans. I'm not sure if I'm supposed to help him with this part, or if I should hope he summons his mental faculties long enough to take a shower. In his current state, a slippery tub seems like the last place he should be, but what choice do we have?

Vince prods his cheek with his fingers. As he becomes aware of the dampness between his legs, his face turns a fierce crimson colour, killing any hope I had of this incident being erased from his memory.

"Did you bite your cheek?" I ask in an effort to divert his attention toward something less humiliating.

He buries his face in his hands. Next thing he'll say is he has a headache and needs to lie down for an hour or twelve. As I bend to pick up my sweater, he mumbles, "Coat."

"Coat?" I repeat. I glimpse the sweater. "Did you want this? To cover up… that?" I indicate his lap.

Vince shakes his head slowly. A faint red smear on his lip answers my previous question about his cheek. "*Cold,*" he says, and makes a motion toward the door, which is standing wide open.

My brain does a rapid inventory of the current situation. Vince is priority number one, and I need to explain what happened to mom before I can confront Trisha. I simply cannot be everywhere at once.

Slipping my hand under Vince's elbow, I guide him to his feet. He brings his fingers close to his face, probing his eyes in a way that suggests he's suffering from an acute postictal headache, until I remember that I removed his glasses and set them on the table.

"Oh! Hang on." I let go of his arm and reach for the glasses, placing them back on his nose as carefully as I can manage. "I didn't want them to break."

The wintery air is still gusting through the house, so I escort him upstairs to bathe and sleep before heading back downstairs to locate Trisha. Parked outside our house, her dad's BMW purrs loudly. Trisha is sitting behind the wheel, staring down at her phone while the heater cooks her alive. I duck into the passenger seat, getting a strong whiff of leather as the door closes behind me. It's positively scorching inside the car, but under dad's coat, I'm shivering.

"Why did you leave?" I ask her. "You're supposed to stay with a person who's having a seizure to make sure they don't hurt themselves."

"Stay with him?" She lowers the phone, pinning me with a glare. "I couldn't stand to watch any of that. It's traumatic."

"Traumatic? Are you serious right now?" My tongue wrestles with the right words. Disbelief streams through my veins until I'm burning with fury. "So, let me get this straight. Your parents are *doctors* and you can't handle seeing Vince have a seizure?"

"Well, you didn't exactly prepare me for this."

She's right; I didn't. But that doesn't matter. When someone is struggling, you stay. "I know. I was going to tell you, but I didn't know how."

"Why do you even want this?" Her voice mixes with the roar of the heater, making the words acerbic. "You don't have to stay with him, Gabby. You're never going to have a normal relationship with Vince."

Looking at Trisha, hearing the words that are spilling out of her mouth… it's like watching Vince convulse on the floor, knowing he's somewhere else, that this isn't him at all.

"I just don't want you to get hurt," she says in a lame attempt to dull the sting of my silence. "And it seems like he's hurting you."

"Vince isn't hurting me… but you are." She opens her mouth to argue as I reach for the door. "You know what, Trish? Go home, before you do any more damage."

"Can I at least come in and get my stuff?"

"I'll bring it to school tomorrow," I reply, and slam the door in her face. I'm halfway up the steps by the time she reaches the road, veering off somewhere into the darkness.

Back inside, I hang up dad's coat and tidy the kitchen table. I stack Trisha's books on the bench next to my backpack, wondering if I was too hard on her or not hard enough. It's not like I didn't panic the first time Vince collapsed. But did I run away? No. I did what the brochures instructed: I kept my cool, even when it felt like the world was going up in flames.

I reach for the bowl of popcorn, but rather than toss it in the trash, I carry it up to the attic. Vince, now showered and dressed, is sitting on his bed, staring down at his glasses in his hands as I emerge from the opening.

"Welcome back," I say.

Vince smiles. "How long…?"

"A couple of minutes. Nowhere near long enough to be an emergency." I jiggle the bowl, rattling the kernels inside. "Are you hungry?"

I sit down on his bed and offer him the popcorn. Vince collects a few pieces and eats them slowly, an empty stare plastered on his face. I follow his gaze, staring at the wall that was never meant to be transcended. And maybe there will always be a wall in our relationship in the form of his epilepsy, but walls can be broken down. As long as we're on the same side, nothing else matters.

"Gabby?"

I look at him, memorizing the angles of his face. "Yes?"

"I'm sorry."

"Don't apologize. You didn't do anything wrong."

"I scared you."

I rest my head on his shoulder, thinking of all the things that could go wrong, like head injuries and sleep seizures and sudden unexpected death. Vince doesn't scare me; his epilepsy does. How much time do I have with him? Even if it was the rest of my life, it wouldn't feel like enough.

"You don't have to do this," he says. His voice thrums through me, giving me the sensation of being underwater. "If you wanted to meet other people, I'd understand."

"I don't want to meet other people." I lift my head. "I've met other people, and they don't come close to you."

"This isn't going to be easy."

I nod. "I know. But it'll be worth it."

He leans his forehead against mine. Somewhere in his skull, the next seizure looms like a distant storm cloud. There's no telling when it will strike or what kind of damage it will do, but we're here now, and we're safe. I pull his mouth down to mine and kiss him deeply, and for the first time, I think he can read my mind.

Chapter 14

For the next three days, I avoid Trisha as much as possible. We have only two classes together—physics and home economics, and she never shows up for the latter—so keeping my distance is easy, or it should be. Trisha and I have been best friends since we were seven years old. Our lives have become so enmeshed that not talking is as painful as addressing our differences. She's the first person I turn to when something goes wrong, so what am I supposed to do now that she's the problem?

At lunchtime, Trisha sits at our usual table with Carla and Elaine. I sit by myself somewhere near the back of the room, trying to be inconspicuous as I pick at my salad. You'd think the whole school knows about our falling out with how everyone keeps looking at me. Not that I care, because when have I ever?

I lift my gaze in time to catch her throwing shade. Carla and Elaine take turns shooting me daggers, although Carla's so sweet that her nasty glances are more like butter knives. Just as I'm about to make a dramatic exit from this overcrowded cafeteria, someone slaps down a tray and takes a seat, blocking my view of the three stooges.

Casey hunches over his food, studying me. His gaze wanders toward Trisha's table before boomeranging back to my face.

"Why aren't you sitting with your friends?" he asks, plucking a tater tot off his plate and popping it into his mouth.

"Why aren't you sitting with *your* friends?" I return.

Casey shrugs. "You looked lonely."

I'm not about to admit he's right, though something in my expression gives me away, judging by the smile that bends his mouth. "I'm not lonely," I say, "just preoccupied."

"Mm-hmm." Casey dunks another tater tot into the pool of ketchup. "Sure you are."

"I don't recall inviting you to sit with me. So why are you here?"

"I'm doing you a favour. Sitting by yourself is bound to attract all kinds of unwanted attention."

"I was just about to leave, actually. You can go back to your table now."

"Sure you were." When Casey leans forward, he completely obscures my view of Trisha. Somehow, I sense he knows this—that it is, in fact, part of his plan. Corner me when I'm feeling defeated, and I'll be putty in his hands.

Since Casey has no intention of leaving, I gather up my tray and cross the room to the row of garbage cans by the door. Out of the corner of my eye, I spot Trisha's neon-coloured beanie. She's out of her seat in a flash, giving me only seconds to calculate the shortest route to my locker. As I step outside, the familiar percussion of her boots echoes in my ears. I'm going to have to face her sooner or later, but right now, I want to be alone.

"Gabby," Trisha says. "Gabby!" Suddenly, her footsteps stop. I keep moving forward, pretending not to notice.

"I know you can hear me," she seethes.

I stop. When I turn around, Trisha is a solid twenty feet away, her dark skin glowing in the fluorescent lights above us. The wrinkles in her forehead smooth away the longer we stare at each other. I give her a chance to catch up, and we walk to my locker in tense silence.

"How's Vince?" Trisha asks when we're almost there.

"Fine. He hasn't had a seizure in a few days."

"That's good, isn't it?"

"Yes."

When we reach my locker, Trisha says, "I wanted to apologize for what I said in the car the other night. I talked to my dad about Vince's seizures, and he said you were right to be mad at me."

"I still am mad at you," I tell her. "Epilepsy isn't contagious. If something bad happened to someone *you* loved, I wouldn't leave."

"I know. I feel awful." Trisha leans her head against the metal door and gives me a contrite smile. "How can I make it up to you?"

I clatter around in the narrow space, noisily rearranging my books. "Just don't let it happen again."

"Deal."

The bell trills, signaling the end of the lunch hour and our conversation. Within seconds, the hallway is bustling with bodies and chatter. Trisha glances back at the cafeteria doors in time to see Carla and Elaine emerging from the hubbub, their faces registering suspicion at the sight of me. Sometimes, all it takes is one bad thing to expose your weakest alliances. Elaine stalks off immediately. Carla, a few paces behind, flicks her eyes between Trisha and me before allowing the movement of the crowd to carry her away.

At last, Trisha faces me and hikes up her backpack. "I should go. I don't want to be late for class."

I almost ask her when getting to class on time became a priority, but I already know the answer. It all started when Vince showed up, and I learned that nothing would ever be the same again.

*

They say every cloud has a silver lining. For mom, the silver lining to Vince no longer being able to drive is that she gets to be my chauffeur again on swim nights. She's waiting for me in the parking lot when I leave school a few hours later, carrying my backpack on one shoulder and my pool bag on the other.

"How was school?" she asks as I climb into the passenger seat and put on my seatbelt.

"Fine." I train my eyes on the car in front of us. If it were Vince asking the question, I'd be more inclined to tell the truth—but if he were here, I wouldn't have reason to be mad at Trisha in the first place.

Mom frowns, cocking her head. "Do you want to talk about it?"

"Do I sound like I'm in a talking mood?"

She sighs. At last, the soccer mom van blocking the driveway makes its turn, and mom creeps forward to check in both directions. It's another reminder of Vince, so I dig out my phone and stare at it until I forget why he isn't here.

Once we leave school property, mom, all dressed up in her puffy winter coat and Toronto Maple Leafs toque, looks over at me again. Her cheeks are rosy and bright from smiling so much. I know she's missed these mother-daughter bonding sessions, but sooner or later, everything changes: people leave, friendships end, and silence replaces conversation. If Vince were here, he'd probably say it's "inevitable," and I would just roll my eyes.

Eventually, mom asks, "How are things with Trisha?"

"I don't know. Fine, I guess."

"Did you get a chance to talk to her?"

What is with moms asking so many questions? "Yeah." I lower my phone, because I can't take not knowing any longer. "How's Vince?"

"Hmm? Oh, he's all right. Your dad has him working outside—nothing too strenuous, of course."

"Trisha's dad said I was right to be mad at her. She's so... *difficult* sometimes."

"She wasn't being difficult. She was afraid."

"Of *Vince*? Because he had a *seizure*?"

"Gabby, try to put yourself in other people's shoes. You and Trisha have been best friends for years and you tell each other everything. But you didn't tell her about this—she found out the hard way. She probably felt helpless, and when people feel helpless, sometimes they behave in ways that don't make sense." Mom steers down the street leading to the rec centre. "People make mistakes. *Friends* make mistakes. And you can choose to either forgive them or forget them, but either way, the decision is up to you."

I can't tell who's rubbed off on whom: if spending so much time around mom turned Vince into some kind of sage, or if all that worldliness followed him here from Oshawa, painting our lives in colours we'd never seen before. Either way, it's too much. They can't always be right about everything, can they?

"Well, I've made it. Trisha and I were growing apart, anyway."

"You can't stay mad at her forever, or you won't have a best friend anymore."

"You give such good advice, mom. You should be a life coach or something."

"I'm going to chalk your sarcasm up to stress and not take that comment personally," she replies, which is exactly what I imagine a life coach would say.

Once we arrive at the rec centre, I head off to the changerooms, leaving mom to make small talk with the woman dad nearly married. A few minutes later, I discover that their conversation has expanded to include one more person: Melanie Hargrave. She's wearing a tomato-red Speedo and dark blue swim cap, both shiny and dripping with water from the pool. When she sees me, my heart freezes in my chest. Swimming is *my* sport, my escape. It's a childish reaction, but after everything that's happened with Vince and Trisha, it would be nice if one thing didn't change.

As I approach the group, Tanya motions to her guest. "Gabby, I'd like you to meet Melanie. She says you two know each other from school."

"We have a bunch of classes together," Melanie supplies, as if it will help jog my memory—as if I could possibly forget the star athlete who put our rinky-dink rural high school on the map.

"I know," I say, switching my focus back to Tanya. "So… what's the plan?"

"Well, you've been working really hard these past few months, and I thought you could test your skills with a little friendly competition."

"Oh, that's a fantastic idea!" mom gushes. "Don't you think so, Gabby?" she adds, because clearly the enthusiasm doesn't show anywhere on my face.

I smile indulgently at her. "I wish I'd thought of it myself."

"Less talking, more swimming," Tanya says. She and mom exchange a few more pleasantries as Melanie and I head for the starting block. Even at school, we only talk when forced into situations requiring us to communicate. Melanie is captain of the volleyball team, a field hockey fiend, and has even found a way to make badminton look dangerous. If she ever noticed me at all, it was only to take pity on my miniscule list of accomplishments.

"Where's your boyfriend?" Melanie asks.

"At home."

"That's probably for the best. Wouldn't want you getting distracted."

We take up our respective positions. Melanie tucks some hair under her cap and rests her right foot against the wedge as she leans down to grasp the front of the block. Her cinnamon brown tan makes me look like a dead fish by comparison, although I'm hoping that once I'm in the water I will magically come back to life.

Tanya sidles up to the pool. In the distance, mom is perched on one of the bleachers, gnawing nervously on her bottom lip.

I pull my goggles down as Tanya asks, "Racers ready?"

"Ready," Melanie quips, rounding her shoulders.

I take a deep breath and hinge forward as well, bringing myself within inches of my reflection. "Ready."

"On my signal—" Tanya raises her left hand. Her right one clutches her whistle and parks it between her lips. As it screams, Melanie and I dive into the water. With both arms extended above my head, all I can see is the sparkling blue of the pool's bottom as I propel myself forward. After a few yards, I reach toward the surface, breaking through with a sharp intake of air. Melanie has managed to keep up—this surprises me. With how good she is, I expected her to be leading.

As the finish line draws near, I raise my elbows over my head, reaching farther with each stroke. My fingers graze the rough surface of the wall seconds before Melanie latches on to the edge of the lane.

Tanya squats in front of me, wearing a smile I've never seen from her before. "See what happens when you don't focus on boys?" Her gaze darts to Melanie, bobbing a few feet away. "What happened?"

My comrade climbs out of the pool. Water sluices off her back and arms, splattering the floor as she struts toward the bench for a towel. She's not humble like Vince, who's practically addicted to congratulating people. And I wish more than anything he could've been here tonight.

Tanya directs her focus back to me. "If you swim like that in a real competition, I'm going to need to find you a better coach."

"Don't hold your breath. Now that Melanie knows I can beat her, she'll stop at nothing to reclaim her throne."

"You have a future, Gabby. A bright one. And you have a choice: either you can start believing in yourself, or you can let people like Melanie hold you back. What's it going to be?"

"I guess I can try believing in myself," I say, knowing how sarcastic it sounds.

Tanya doesn't flinch. Instead, she nods and gestures to the pool, where the waves are still crashing back and forth, pushing my body this way and that.

"In that case, I want to see you do the 50-meter freestyle in thirty-five seconds or less *consistently*. Let's say three times in a row to start."

"That's inhumane."

"Then I'll get Melanie over here and you can race her three times instead."

"You wouldn't."

"I would."

How utterly heartless. "Fine, I'll do three thirty-fives. But only because my mom is here."

After she walks away, I linger in the water, wrestling with this latest quandary. A bright future. A better coach. All those opportunities will have to come at a cost, and I'm afraid of what that cost might be. Vince. The farm. Mom and dad. Even Ryan, whom I spend most of my days trying to avoid. Am I truly prepared to give it all up?

An hour later, Tanya blows her whistle for the last time and I exit the pool with a dull cramp under each arm. I'm used to being tired after swim practice, but *in pain* is a new feeling. Like when Vince first arrived and my room felt like a prison instead of a sanctuary. I'll get used to it, but before that, I'll wonder why I ever agreed to something so ridiculous.

Mom beats a direct path to me, a thick, white towel draped over her arm. As soon as I'm swaddled in its warmth, she reels me in for a hug, saying, "You have no idea how much I needed this."

I'm not sure if she's referring to the spontaneous embrace or the fleeting illusion of normalcy, but she's right: I've needed this, too. "Let's go home. I want to tell Vince about how I kicked Melanie's butt."

"Are you sure you should be rubbing this in his face?"

"How am I rubbing it in his face? If Vince were here, he'd be telling me how amazing I am."

She presses her lips together. Two days ago, I caught her thumbing through the epilepsy brochures and making notes in her diary. Despite my apprehensions about Vince's future with us, my parents have been trying to understand his disorder and shape our lives around his needs. If that doesn't make Vince feel better, then knowing he was right about me should do the trick.

"I know you want to share these exciting moments with Vince— and you absolutely should," mom adds hastily, "but try not to overdo it. Things have been difficult for all of us lately."

"I know." I falter. "Mom?"

"Hmm?"

"Do you think I have a bright future?"

She looks startled. "Of course I do. I always have. Why would you ask that?"

"Tanya said I might need a better coach, if I decide to swim competitively on a regular basis."

"Well, if you trust your coach to tell you when you're doing something wrong, you should also trust her to know when you're on the right path. Although more advanced training may not be in our budget right now."

"That's what I thought."

"But I don't want you to let that stop you. If you want to swim, then we'll find a way to make it work—sell the farm if we have to."

"I don't want you to sell the farm." As much as I hate the early mornings, grumble about the workload, and worry about smelling like manure, the farm is still home to me. I'm not sure any dream is worth giving up such a key part of who I am.

"Then we'll think of something else."

Mom walks me to the changerooms. Before I go inside, I turn to her and say, "I'm glad you're here, even if you embarrass me in front of my coach."

"What are moms for?" She kisses my cheek, then marches toward the stands practically bursting with pride.

Chapter 15

Christmas always involves a lot of yelling in our house. It started when Ryan was a baby and hadn't yet grasped the concept of words, leaving long, piercing vowels as his sole means of communication. Sometimes, he'd scream at the lights, twinkling endlessly in the bows of the tree. Other times, it was Santa himself that sent my brother into convulsions of terror. Now, Ryan's hollering for a brand new reason: he's playing Joseph in his school's Christmas play, meaning he has to wear a beard that itches like a nest of spiders. In any case, it will most definitely not be a silent night.

"Hold still," mom commands, sticking more tape to Ryan's cheek. "Unless you want me to get the glue."

"No!"

"That's what I thought." She sees me standing in the doorway and says, "Are you here to help me, or are you just watching?"

"Watching. It's way more fun."

She turns back to my brother, sitting on the bathroom counter dressed in a brown cloak and wool socks. He scratches furiously at the strip of tape on his cheek and mumbles, "Why can't I be Mary?"

"Because Mary's a woman," mom says. "Besides, you'd have to hold baby Jesus."

"It would be better than wearing an itchy beard."

"Grown men have beards. Don't you want people to treat you like a grown up?" I ask.

Ryan considers this, then tells me, "Vince doesn't have a beard."

"Yes, he does. It's pale, so you can't see it."

"No, he doesn't." Ryan rubs his nose with the back of his hand, mixing some snot in with the reddish brown material.

I set my jaw. Mom's nearly finished fighting with the beard, so I tell her, "I'm going to go take the cookies out of the oven."

My feet tread noiselessly down the stairs, drawn by the glow of the decorations and the warmth of the fire. Vince is unwrapping a length of mermaid-green garland from one of the boxes dad brought upstairs. For the past couple of weeks, he went back and forth on the decision to return home for Christmas, saying it had been months since he'd seen his family and they would be disappointed if he didn't show. Then his sister, Natalie, announced she'd be spending the holidays abroad with some friends, while his stepdad planned to take the younger kids on an impromptu trip to Montreal, leaving his mom, Edna, and sister, Lillian, to celebrate in their own way (a manicure followed by a trip to the bookstore). So, Vince decided to stay and observe Christmas with us. Deep down, I think this is what he wanted all along, and so did I.

"Where do you normally put the garland?" he asks me.

"Around the banister." I take the metallic rope from his hands and wrap one end of it around the newel post, then thread it through the gaps between the spindles all the way up the staircase. Once that's done, I return to the living room, where Vince is sitting on the couch, quietly taking it all in. The stockings above the fireplace. Mom's collection of glass angels. The paper snowflakes taped to the window. And me, standing on the stairs, wearing a sweater that's a tad too warm for the current temperature of the room.

"What now?" Vince asks.

"Now," I reply, heading for the kitchen, "we take the cookies out to cool so we can ice them later."

He follows me toward the oven, watching as I slip on a pair of mitts and remove the tray. Twelve undressed gingerbread men fill the room with fragrance. My mouth waters as I set them on the stove and tuck my hands under my arms to quell the urge to snatch one up.

Vince pours each of us a glass of eggnog and sets them on the table. "I wonder how Natalie's doing," he says conversationally.

"Better than I am," I reply without thinking.

Vince extends his hand, grasping my fingers, and reels me into my usual seat. Mom's still keeping us busy, but tomorrow is Christmas Eve and you're supposed to be close to the ones you love. I take a seat, and my knee bumps his not-so-accidentally.

"She's so far from home," he continues, "I worry about her."

"And yet, you loathe when people worry about you."

His brow quirks. "You hate that word."

"What, loathe?"

"Yes."

"Well, maybe I'm expanding my vocabulary. See? I'm not as learning-averse as you think."

Vince chuckles, skimming my knuckles with his thumb.

Mom and Ryan appear. They've managed to keep the beard on Ryan's face using Scotch tape and sheer will, and he's even tolerating the baggy wool cloak, cinched around his waist using a stitch of baling twine from the barn. As soon as he sees the cookies, he sprints toward the stove, waving his hands above his head to free them from the impositions of the heavy sleeves.

"Not so fast," Vince warns, "they're still scorching hot."

"I don't care," Ryan snaps.

Mom grabs him by the arm, saying, "Well, I do. I worked too hard on your costume to waste the evening in the hospital." She addresses me. "You're sure you don't want to come?"

"As devastated as I am that I won't be able to watch Ryan scratch his face off, I really think I should stay and help Vince. Just in case there's an emergency with the cows."

"I doubt anything will happen. If you want to go, then you should." Vince takes a sip of his eggnog. He knows I'm worried about his safety, even though the odds of him having a seizure are low right now. "Don't let me ruin your fun," he says, almost as an afterthought.

"You couldn't if you tried."

Through the kitchen window, I spot dad making his way toward the house after completing some last-minute checks in the barn. The cows' welfare is always front and centre in his mind, since our livelihood depends on them. He's left Vince in charge of looking after the place while he and mom are at Ryan's school, watching the fifth-grade Christmas play and taking a much-needed break from caring for Vince.

Mom starts bundling Ryan into his coat and boots. The beard snags on the zipper, making Ryan yelp. As much as I'm enjoying the show, mom seems far from amused, so I pack a few gingerbread cookies into a container and stuff Ryan's head into a toque.

"Here," I say, sticking the cookies in his hands. "For the road."

Ryan examines the biscuits steaming up the Tupperware. "There's no icing," he snarls.

"Use your imagination."

Mom has nearly finished dressing herself when she turns to me and her face adopts a shadowy expression. "Are you going to be okay?"

"Of course." She waits, expecting further reassurance. "I have a ton of homework to keep me occupied."

There it is: the sigh of relief. "We should be home around eight. There's chili in the freezer if you two are hungry, important phone numbers are on the fridge, and if there's an emergency—"

"I'll call you right away," I say, my voice lowered. Vince has gone back to the living room to feed the fire, and Ryan is too distracted by his festive treat to pay heed.

She smiles, sliding her purse onto her shoulder. "Great. Well." Turning to my brother, she takes a breath and says, "Time to go. Dad's waiting in the truck."

"Bye, Gabby," Ryan says as they bustle out the door, "have fun kissing your boyfriend."

Mom says, "By the way, it's supposed to get icy tonight. Don't forget to salt the steps."

"Okay, I'll let Vince know."

Mom and Ryan climb into dad's truck. After taking a couple of minutes to get settled, dad puts the Ford in reverse and backs a wide circle toward the driveshed. The tires squeak over the fresh snow as they drive away, off to enjoy a long night of flashing cameras and forgotten lines. I wave until they're out of sight, then shut the door and make my way into the living room, where I find Vince sitting on the sofa. I cave in the cushion on his left, and we stare into the flickering flames in silence, letting our aloneness solidify in the empty spaces.

"Now what?" he says.

I bite my lip, trying not to blurt out the first thought that fills my brain. "We could watch a movie."

He picks up the remote and switches on the TV. The room is engulfed in flashes of light, the colours so sharp they cast shadows on the wall. I don't even realize I've turned to stone until Vince says, "It's okay—I'm not photosensitive."

My shoulders relax. "What normally triggers them?"

"It depends. Low blood sugar, stress, sometimes being sick."

"Me?"

Vince's gaze finds mine. "No. Never you."

The TV manages to capture our attention for a full three minutes before we get lost in each other's faces, kissing and kissing and trying not to suffocate. Years of swimming have given me the advantage of greater lung capacity, but Vince is equally used to going without oxygen because of his seizures, which occasionally turn his lips blue. As this visual sneaks into my thoughts, my lips go slack and I pull away, unable to explain why I've suddenly lost interest.

Vince opens his eyes. "What's wrong?"

"Nothing."

"Is it... me?"

I tug at a thread on the sofa's armrest, thinking about what Trisha said a few weeks ago. I knew from the moment I started falling that Vince had the power to carve holes in my heart that are doomed to go unfilled by future partners. Discovering he suffers from a debilitating neurological disorder only deepened my fear of losing him. A similar monologue seems to be circulating in Vince's mind, for he leans back against the sofa and stares down at his hands, like our love is a tiny, featherless chick he risks crushing if he tries to hold on to it too tightly.

"Am I your first?" I ask suddenly.

"My first what?"

I look over at him, watching the light from the screen dance on his skin. "Girlfriend."

"No." Vince shifts. "You're my third."

"Third?" I can handle being second—better than Melanie can, anyway—but third is a bronze medal, barely worthy of acknowledgment. "But I thought you said you got turned down a lot."

"I did, when I was younger. Your two forerunners are relatively recent."

"How recent?"

I can't tell if it's the program we're watching, Vince's embarrassment, or a combination of the two that turns his cheeks red. Just when I think I'm starting to know him, another layer begs to be peeled away. His depth is infinite, and so are his secrets.

"I broke up with my girlfriend in June. Her name was Diana Thorn. We'd been dating for a year. We weren't terribly serious." I picture each fact as a bullet point on a list of unknown length. I keep coming back to the *terribly serious* part, because although it aligns with Vince's manner of speech, it's incredibly vague, especially considering they were together for a year and I'm just hearing about it now.

"And before that?" I prompt him, resting my elbow on the back of the couch and pinning my head on my hand. "Who was your first?"

"Candace Richmond. We only dated for six weeks."

"Were you terribly serious with her?" I can't keep the edge out of my voice.

Vince grins, allaying my fears. "We dated for six weeks," he says again. "You do the math."

"Well, Vince, I didn't realize you were such a player. Here I was thinking you were a nerdy kid who scared away potential dates with your dangerously high expectations, when in reality, you had girls lining up around the block for the privilege of being your girlfriend."

"It's not like that. Yes, I've dated, but the feelings I have for you are brand new to me. Exciting."

More vague language. Fear and excitement are neighbours; your nerves don't know the difference. "It doesn't matter. I'm still not your first."

"Firsts are overrated. Think of the first time you rode a bike. It was scary, right?"

"I guess."

"And it took some practice, before you felt comfortable enough to cycle around the block by yourself."

I envision Vince practicing all kinds of things on Diana and Candace. Holding hands. Bumping knees. Kissing. So much kissing, I can taste his exes and suddenly need a drink.

"Do you want some more eggnog?" I ask as I head for the kitchen.

"Are we done talking?"

"About your past girlfriends? Yes, please." I bend into the fridge for the carton and fill both glasses to the brim. As Vince walks in, I say, "Oh, I almost forgot to tell you: mom says it's getting icy outside, so you'll need to salt the porch tonight."

He nods obediently. Things were simpler when he was the hired hand and I was the farmer's daughter. When we were wolves who stuck to our territories and stayed off one another's hunting ground. I offer Vince his glass and he drains it in a few gulps, then places the dish in the sink and approaches the door, where his coat and boots await.

"We're getting low on firewood," he tells me, slipping into the coat. "I think there's more in the driveshed. Do you want me to bring it in?"

The lines are blurring again. I take a sip of my drink, letting it wash away the dregs of Diana and Candace and who-knows-who-else, before answering, "Sure. Mom and dad would appreciate that."

He nods again, then opens the door and treks across the driveway to the shed. The snow has begun to melt in random spots, spawning silvery patches of ice that ripple in the moonlight. Minutes pass; I start to worry. Eventually, some movement near the driveshed door puts my fears to rest, and Vince retraces his steps to the house bearing an armload of split logs.

I run out the door when I hear the first one clatter onto the ground. He's fallen forward, but his legs are bent and his hands move independently. Not a seizure, just plain bad luck this time.

"Oh, my god." I can practically see the words take shape in the air. "Are you okay?"

Vince has a hand to his head, the other trying to peg his weight so he can stand up. "I think so. You weren't kidding about the ice."

Great. So this is the second time—no, third—that he's fallen down and I haven't caught him. No wonder I'm his third girlfriend. "Here, let me help you up."

As I pull him to his feet, he winces in pain. I stare at his hand, clamped tightly over his right brow, and my stomach lurches in familiar helplessness. My fingers are frozen raw as I reach for his face and peel back the protective layer he's applied. The skin is shiny underneath. Even in near total darkness, there's no mistaking fresh blood.

He must notice the shock on my face, or feel the warm ooze of his wound. Vince lowers his hand and stares at his palm. Starts swaying like he's going to faint. I'm prepared this time and grab his arm before he can fall.

"It's okay," I say, "let's get you inside."

We enter the kitchen and cut a beeline to the powder room without taking off our boots. Geometric fragments of snow litter the hardwood floor. As I reach for the light switch, Vince says, "I'll clean that up."

"No. You're going to sit down and let me take care of you."

He comes within an inch of protesting. My stomach gives a faint tug of warning as I direct him to sit on the lid of the toilet and gingerly pry away his fingers to assess the damage.

"Oh—"

"Let me see." When he tries to stand, I push him back into a sitting position. He scowls. "It's *my* face."

"Sit," I say through clenched teeth. The skin above his brow is split like a microwaved hotdog. Blood is gushing into his eye and his hair is sticky and matted. The unmistakable copper smell burrows deep into my nose until I'm forced to turn away.

Vince takes the opportunity to stand up. He leans toward the mirror, smearing a red handprint on the sink as he tries to steady himself.

"Here." I jam my hand into the box of tissues and pull out a wad of sheets. Vince presses the tissue ball to his injury and sucks an involuntary breath between his teeth. "Keep pressure on it."

"I'm trying. They're too thin."

I dig all the way to the bottom of the box and hand him what's left. "I'll go get more. You should sit down."

Once Vince is settled, I race into the kitchen and rummage through the cupboard under the sink for the paper towels. I sacrifice a few sheets to the mess on the floor, tossing five or six of the absorbent squares behind me like breadcrumbs before fashioning a series of makeshift compresses out of what remains on the roll. What Vince needs is proper medical care from a licensed physician, not shoddy first aid by a teenage girl who occasionally sticks a Band-Aid on her little brother's knees.

"We need to go to the hospital. You need stitches," I say as he arranges the compress on his head.

"I'm not going."

"Vince—"

"I'm *not going*." The paper towels seem to be working, but Vince doesn't dare move his hand.

I steel myself, channeling mom into every word. "Vincent McCarthy, you are going to the hospital and that's that."

He bends forward, placing his elbows on his knees. For the longest time, we're both silent, lost in the words we can't say. While I wait for Vince to come to his senses, I wipe the blood off the sink and mop the melted snow off the floor. If I'd just gone to the stupid play, Vince wouldn't have felt the need to fetch more firewood to thaw my frosty personality, and I wouldn't be trying to figure out how to get a grown man to do what he's told.

After I've dried the floors, I march back to the bathroom. Vince's cheeks are pale and he's fighting to stay awake. I whip out my phone and start dialing 911. He clamps his fingers on my wrist, his gaze wide and piercing as it focuses on my face.

"Gabby, I'm not going," he says, his voice hoarse. "Please."

"You know, for such a smart guy, you're being incredibly stupid right now," I snap.

"I can't ride in an ambulance. The stress of it will send me over the edge."

"I'd argue that's the best place for you to have a seizure!"

He raises his hand imploringly. "If you really love me, you'll respect my wishes."

The shock of his words hits me. I can't speak, though I make a few sputtering noises in my attempt to express my anger. *How dare you?* I want to scream. *Of course I love you. I always have. And if you love* me, *you'll let me help you.*

My fingers lock on his elbow. "Let's go."

"What?"

"I'm taking you to the hospital."

The last bit of colour drains from his skin, taking his strength with it. "You can't drive."

"I can drive the tractor. How different can a truck be?"

With Vince more or less upright, I lead him through the house, out the door, and across the driveway to the shed. Dad's taken me out a couple of times to practice, but we always stick to the gravel roads and never exceed fifty kilometres an hour. Besides, what's the point in having a spare vehicle if you never put it to use?

I help Vince climb into the passenger seat. The musty smell of old seats and dusty gages mingles with the metallic fetor of clotting blood. He fades in and out of consciousness for a minute before suddenly coming to and gazing around at his surroundings in horror.

"It's okay," I assure him as I lift the key off the rearview mirror, "I know what I'm doing."

"You can't drive," he argues.

"Yeah, well, neither can you right now."

I turn the key, firing up the engine. The wheel is ice-cold and I cling to it for dear life. *It's just like driving the tractor*, I tell myself. What would dad say about driving the tractor? *Go slowly.* I shift into drive and ease my foot off the brake, propelling us into the moon-soaked night.

"Lights," Vince murmurs.

"What?"

"Your headlights… aren't on."

I fumble around in the dark, bothering all the controls, until Vince finally reaches over and switches on the correct one. The light beams off the mounds of snow flanking the driveway. The rest is up to me. Vince's safety is in my hands, and I'm going to guard it with my life.

We bump along the thick blanket of snow and ice. A heavy mist swirls in the headlights. I keep my hands glued to the wheel, my eyes fixed on the road, and my breath locked in my chest. Beside me, Vince has his head tipped back against the seat. The tires skid on the slippery patches, making the truck fishtail from one side of the road to the other and back again.

"You're driving too fast," Vince says.

"It's an emergency."

"Gabby, slow down."

I hit the brake, and the truck responds by sliding sideways, almost into the ditch.

"Steer in," Vince barks, "steer *in*."

"Into *what*?"

His hand grabs the wheel. The backend of the truck is still zigzagging out behind us, but we seem to be slowing down.

"This was a terrible idea," Vince tells me. I start to wonder if he's right, if I should've called mom and dad and let them handle this instead, when he says, "But you're the only person I know who's brave enough to attempt it."

I don't feel brave at all. But maybe courage is something only other people can see. "How's your head?"

"Pounding like a drum."

"We're almost at the hospital." My foot presses down on the accelerator, and the needle climbs slowly over seventy. "How am I doing?" I ask conversationally.

"Surprisingly well. I suppose those tractor-driving lessons paid off." As the lights of the town break through the trees, Vince adds, "Am I right to assume you're going to tell your father about this?"

"The driving, or the fall?"

"Both."

The truck judders over a pothole, forcing my grip on the wheel to tighten. "I have to, even if it means I'll lose my driving privileges for life."

For the remainder of the trip, Vince and I say nothing. When we arrive at the hospital, I pull into an empty space in the corner of the parking lot and guide Vince through the automatic doors. The ladies working behind the counter are all around mom's age, with the exception of the nurse who steps out to examine Vince and urge him into a wheelchair. He sounds drowsy as he tells them about the fall, how long ago it happened, and that he has epilepsy, in case it makes a difference to his treatment. Before long, he's taken into one of the rooms behind the desk, leaving me standing by myself in the hallway.

One of the ladies asks me, "Is there someone we can call for you?"

My voice comes out as a rasp. "My dad, Augustus O'Connor."

I give them dad's number, knowing full well he's in no position to rush out and save me, but I don't know what else to do. I must've broken a dozen laws tonight, not to mention dad's trust. But I couldn't let Vince down. Not again.

Fifteen minutes later, dad comes barreling through the doors and surveys the waiting room in a panic. I swallow, trying to dislodge the egg-sized lump in my throat as his gaze settles on me, but his face is devoid of reproach. In his eyes, all I see is fear.

Dad swerves around a row of chairs to approach me. He smells the way he always does, like old plaid and fresh hay, as he takes the seat next to mine. "Gabby, are you okay?"

"I'm fine. It's Vince…"

"Another seizure?"

I shake my head. "He fell. I know I should've called an ambulance, but…" I look down at my boots. "I took the truck instead."

"The spare truck? You mean the one you don't have a license to drive yet?" I nod, prompting dad to say, "We'll discuss the consequences of that choice later. Where's Vince?"

"They already took him in. He was bleeding a lot. They wanted to make sure he doesn't have a concussion."

"That makes sense. Did he call his parents?"

"I don't think so." Knowing Vince, he'll delay the inevitable for as long as possible. What would Natalie say if she knew where her brother was in this moment? I bet she'd be a lot more composed than I am. Then again, she's probably accompanied Vince to the hospital more times than I can count.

The nurse assigned to Vince's care rounds the corner and makes her way to where dad and I are sitting. "Mr. O'Connor?"

"That's me," dad replies, looking concerned.

"Mr. McCarthy is asking for you."

"I'll be right there." Dad turns to me again and forces himself to smile, like he wants me to believe everything's going to be okay. "Your mom's waiting in the truck with Ryan. Why don't you go warm up? I'll drive the spare truck home." He extends his palm toward me, and I relinquish the keys without comment.

Dad dutifully follows the nurse to the place beyond the counter, where Vince and countless others are awaiting care. It could be hours before he's released, and I know dad won't let me stay, so I pluck up my courage and make my way to the doors. Mom is sitting in the passenger seat, her face waxy and grey in the light of the nearby lamppost. When she sees me approaching in the side mirror, she rolls down the window and waits for me to come clean.

"Vince had a bad fall. It was the ice this time. Dad's in there with him. He's going to drive the spare truck home." The longer I talk, the softer my voice becomes, until I'm whispering the last part.

Mom sighs. "You're shivering. Climb in the back with Ryan."

As I'm enveloped by the truck's warmth, Ryan gazes around in bewilderment. The tape has left red marks on his cheeks. At his feet lies the empty cookie container. It could be a normal December night, if not for where we're sitting.

"Where's Vince?" my brother asks, scratching his face.

I don't answer. Ryan's never seen Vince suffer a seizure, but he's old enough to know what epilepsy is. And if Vince gets to be a part of our family, maybe it's time I started treating my brother like an adult instead of a kid dressed up in a fake beard.

"He's talking to a doctor. He had a bad fall." I add, "I was really scared because Vince has epilepsy, and sometimes the seizures can cause him to hurt himself. But he's going to be okay—he just needs a few stitches."

"I saw someone have a seizure once," Ryan says, taking me by surprise. "Mr. P showed us a video in health class during First Aid Week."

"Oh. So, you know what to do?" I ask, ready to correct him.

I picture the map of Canada, with its provinces and territories neatly coloured and properly labelled, suggesting that my brother knows more about the world than I give him credit for. He kicks disappointedly at the Tupperware and says, "You're supposed to stay with someone having a seizure—and you're not supposed to restrain them."

"That's right."

"Did you know that anyone can have a seizure? Not just people with epilepsy."

I do, but I pretend I don't so he can feel that button-busting pride I felt the first time I plowed the driveway solo. "I didn't know that. Anyone?"

"Yup. Seizures are super common." He suddenly dissolves into a fit of impatience that proves he's still my whiny, annoying little brother, despite his occasional flashes of brilliance. "Can we go home now?"

"Soon," mom replies. Her eyes go to the mirror again. From the backseat, I see dad approaching the truck and hold my breath, expecting the worst.

Mom steps out of the passenger seat. Once she's outside, I can't hear their conversation, but I can probably guess what they're talking about. And I have a feeling I'm not going to like it.

Our family splits up. As the hospital fades to a speck in the rearview mirror, I try to imagine Macbeth's dilemma and how the story might've changed if he hadn't been so obsessed with dethroning King Duncan. Sometimes wanting something is more powerful than actually having it, because it's what we choose to do that makes us who we are.

Personally, if I could do tonight over, I wouldn't change anything at all.

Chapter 16

As punishment for driving the truck without a license, dad has designed a new chore schedule. My days begin at 5AM on the front porch, where I'm expected to partake in a shovel-and-salt ritual regardless of whether it snowed the night before. After that, at 5:30, I march up to the barn and feed the cows until 6:15, at which time I return to the house and prepare breakfast for the human inhabitants. Since there's no school until the new year, there's no break from the work until 6:30PM, when cooler heads prevail and mom steps in as the head of the house (and the dinner table).

The worst part of all this is that I'm not allowed to talk to Vince, other than to inform him of meals or emergencies. When we're not busy ghosting each other or eating lunch at separate times, we're lying in total silence in the attic, painfully aware of every breath coming and going between us. If Vince had a phone, it would be a different game. But he doesn't, so at night, I write my thoughts on Post-Its and stick them to the wall like five-second love letters. By the end of the week, my half of the room is a mosaic of confessions.

Vince's is bare.

I thunder down to the kitchen. When I get there, dad is swishing soapy water around the coffee pot—a job normally assigned to our hired hand.

"Where's Vince?" I ask from the doorway.

Dad empties the pot into the sink, rinses it, and sets it back on the hotplate before drying his hands. "He went home."

"You sent him away," I say, jumping to the only logical conclusion I can come up with, the one I desperately want to believe. "And you didn't even talk to me, you just did it."

My father, with his silvery spill of hair and heavy plaid jacket, turns away from the sink. He slips his hands into his pockets and leans against the edge of the counter, letting the pause in our conversation stretch into a silence that blankets the room.

Finally, dad says, "I didn't send him away. Vince left on his own."

"When?"

"This morning, before you got up. He came to me last night and said he was thinking of going to see his family. He didn't say how long he'd be gone, or if he'd be coming back."

Each of dad's words hits me like a miniature shockwave. Last summer, right before he left for Kingston, I went over to Jayden's house to help him pack. His bedroom was barren, the dresser drawers hollow and musty-smelling. I sat on the bed and handed him shirt after shirt, until all I could smell was the Apple Blossom laundry detergent and his Axe body spray, so permanent in the air that his leaving felt like an illusion. We didn't talk much. I was afraid that opening my mouth would invite a tidal wave into my lungs and I'd drown before he ever knew how I felt about us. Even now, I can't bring myself to respond. All I can do is become the water. I let Vince's absence pass right through me, the force of it insignificant. I remind myself to breathe.

Dad says, "I'm sorry, Gabby. We knew he wasn't planning to stay here indefinitely."

"I know." I look past dad's shoulder to the shimmering mounds of freshly laid snow. Plenty to shovel. "I'll get started on the porch."

"Good girl." Dad picks up his coffee mug and heads to his office to do computer work. There's nothing left to do in the barn. No one left to supervise. Our house returns to a state of unsettled silence, but in my head, I'm screaming.

Vince, the boy with all the words, left without even saying goodbye.

*

As winter drags on, Trisha and I go back to hanging out on a regular basis. Sometimes we let Elaine join us, but she's usually busy trying to prove that the chemistry she has with Ethan is purely of the Bunsen-burner-and-safety-goggles variety, lest anyone doubt her undying hatred toward him. I find plenty of ways to stay occupied myself, from preparing for exams to practicing my breaststrokes, just as I would have done if Vince hadn't been a part of our lives.

I take a sip of my iced tea and point to my phone screen, where Trisha and I are watching a video of the women's Olympic swimming event. Eight competitors are lined up at the end of a dazzlingly clear pool, ready to dive into the 50-meter freestyle. Tanya will be happy to know the solution to my recurring boy troubles involves watching women in Speedos cutting up the lane.

"You see her?" I point to Paulette Klein, from Team Canada, as she rockets into the water. "She's got the best technique. See how she looks directly at the bottom of the pool when she swims?"

"God, I'd be so bored. How do you stand it?" Trisha asks.

I wait until Paulette reaches the finish line before answering, "Swimming's the only thing I can control. Being in control isn't boring."

Trisha pinches some roast beef out of her sandwich. She hates water almost as much as she loathes the cold, but since Vince left us, she's been exceedingly tolerant of my aquatic ambitions, watching video after video as I attempt to drown out my pain.

"Who's that?" She points to a the only black swimmer in the lineup.

"Adelaide Johnson. She's pretty good too, especially in the 100-meter backstroke." I pull up a video of Adelaide rowing to a cool second place during the 2016 Olympic Games in Rio de Janeiro, which holds Trisha's focus until Elaine storms over to us.

"Oh, my god," she says, slamming down her bag on the stairs. "You won't believe what Ethan did this time."

"Don't care, watching swimming," Trisha says, tearing off another shred of roast beef.

I glance up from my phone to see Elaine pacing the stairwell like a deranged animal, her face flushed a murderous pink. Elaine's temper isn't much of a secret around here, but you never know what's going to set her off or how far she'll go to send a message.

"You don't care?" she practically spits. "Well, you should, because Dickbrains Mackenzie just accused me of cheating on last week's test."

"Why would he do that?" I ask.

"Because he's a dick," Elaine deadpans, as if it should be obvious. "And because the thought of a girl—a *blonde* girl, no less—getting better grades in university-level chemistry is apparently a death knell to his cancerous ego."

"Truly dickish behaviour," Trisha agrees.

"Exactly. So now, Mr. Meyers has to investigate the claim, even though he knows I don't have to cheat because I'm the smartest person in the class. Fuck!" she shrieks, the word echoing off the walls.

Trisha reaches into her bag and hands her water bottle to Elaine. "The world would be a hundred times better if men didn't exist," she says as Elaine gulps it down. "Wouldn't you agree, Gabby?"

"Maybe not *all* men," I reply, because it would suck to lose dad (and Ryan, even though I can picture future girlfriends screaming in a stairwell over some dickish thing he did with absolutely no trouble at all).

"Ninety-seven percent of them have got to go," Elaine states, crinkling the bottle, "trust me, I did the math."

And just like that, I'm thinking about Vince. There's a fifty percent chance I still care about him. The odds of him coming back after everything that's happened between us are statistically far lower.

Trisha's voice pulls me back into the conversation. "So, what are you going to do?"

Elaine's brows knot. "Murder is plotted in secret, kitten. But it's going to be well-deserved, in Ethan's case." She hands the empty bottle to Trisha and picks up her bag. "I better go. Have fun fighting over the least dickish guy in school." She pulls open the door, and within moments, she's swept away by the current of bodies.

Trisha turns to me. "I don't think it would be a fair fight."

"Why? Because I'm a swimmer and your idea of exercise is skipping class?"

"No. Because the least dickish guy doesn't go to this school." Her gaze finds mine and holds it until I look away. "Have you heard from him?"

"No."

"Well, maybe he'll come back. You guys are endgame, remember?" Trisha stuffs the sandwich wrapper into her bag and stands up. "I need to talk to Mr. Berkley about a few things. I'll tell him you said hi."

After she disappears, I turn my focus back to the swimmers in my phone. With time and practice, you can train your body to do almost anything—ride a bike, swim straight lines, pass a physics test. If I keep my head down, I'm sure I can learn to forget about Vince.

*

The bus spits me out at the foot of our driveway a few hours later. Even though Vince has been gone for three weeks, I still expect to see him in one of the fields, helping dad fix some fences or check on a sick cow. Instead, there's only an infinite spectrum of greys, from the slush that lines the soles of my boots to the linty accumulation of clouds threatening snow in the distance. In a couple of months, the trees will start budding and life will unfreeze itself from this moment. A fresh start for all of us.

I open the front door, remove my boots, and head straight up to my room with my backpack—something I started doing after Vince left. In his absence, the attic has regained some of its sanctity, although the wall is a cruel reminder of how things used to be. Mom and Ryan are out getting groceries, so it'll be my job to help put everything away. My job to help prepare dinner. To wash dishes. To tutor Ryan. To hold our household together.

The stairs creak underfoot, loud as ever in the vacant shell of our home. Even before I reach the top step, a certain smell hits me—some kind of fabric softener, I think.

Mom doesn't use fabric softener.

After Vince left, I took down all the Post-Its from my side of the wall, scrunched them into tiny paper flowers, and threw them in the trash. Using only a few words per sheet, I'd somehow managed to tell our story. Wrote an essay about us and bled the pen dry. Then I scrapped it, tore the truth to pieces before it could condemn me to a life of lies. But you can only hide from the truth as long as no one else knows about it.

The Post-Its litter the bed in dull pops of colour, the notes flattened to readability. One by one, Vince takes the sheets out of the trash can, skims them, and adds them to the pile. I must seem insane to him, scribbling like a mad woman in the dead of night. Another Post-It, a blue one, unfurls in his fingers, revealing its secrets by the dying light of afternoon.

"You came back," I whisper.

His eyes snap to where I'm standing. His hair is shorter. The Band-aid from his fall, gone. But then he smiles and nothing has changed.

Vince stands up and faces me. "Of course I came back." He holds out the blue Post-It. "I don't think I was meant to read this one."

"You weren't meant to read any of them." I take the note from him. It says: *I worry about losing you every day.*

"I suppose your fears were justified," he says.

"*Are* justified," I correct him. I gesture vaguely to our surroundings. "What are you doing here?"

"I asked your father if I could come back. He said I could, on one condition." Vince pauses. "You."

"Me? As in, as long as I was okay with it?"

"Are you?"

I smile tentatively. "Of course I am. But… I don't understand why you left so suddenly. Even Jayden had the decency to tell me where he was going."

"I know. I guess I was being selfish, like when I didn't tell you about my epilepsy. I couldn't bear the thought of seeing you upset."

"Hiding the truth doesn't stop people from being upset, Vince. If anything, it makes everything worse." I hand him back the Post-It. "I kept worrying about you."

"I was worried about you, too. The first few days at home were difficult…" Before he can elaborate, Vince indicates my bag and says, "But I shouldn't burden you with my problems. It looks like you have a lot of homework."

Freeing my arms from the straps, I let my backpack crash to the floor with my usual carelessness and smirk. Now that Vince is back, there's no need to pretend to be someone I'm not or stretch myself thin to cover his absence. My feet move toward the bed and I pick up one of the Post-Its, tracing its creases with my thumb. I had more to say to Vince in that week of silence than all the months preceding it. As I lower myself onto the bed and gather up the evidence of those sleepless nights, Vince takes a seat beside me and selects a couple notes at random, making my stomach clench in fear.

"You know, a diary would be more private," he says.

"I know. But I didn't expect you to go dumpster diving." I look at him. "What were you doing on my side of the wall, anyway?"

"Seeing things from your perspective. I had no real intention of snooping. I was admiring your metal, and I happened to look down and see all these colourful notes in your trash. I know I should've left them alone. But…"

"But you couldn't help yourself."

"If you had the opportunity to get to know someone better, even at the expense of their privacy, would you do it?"

Warmth floods my face. I wonder if Vince knows how many times I've flipped through his sketchbook, getting our fingerprints mixed up on the graphite-strewn pages. Animals are among his favourite subjects, and the most widely available. His still life drawings are incredible, too. But enfolded within the creamy sheets is an image I never expected to find: a portrait of me in black-and-white, my features slightly smudged and my dark curls practically springing off the page. It was recent, too. So, I guess I wasn't the only one suffering in silence that week.

Vince reads one of the Post-Its out loud. "'I'm sorry I didn't catch you that day.'" He turns to me quizzically. "Which day was that?"

"The first time you had a seizure," I reply quietly. "I saw you stop walking. You were staring off into space and I didn't know what you were looking at. But then you fell and…" I take a breath. "I thought I caused it."

"You didn't. I hadn't had a seizure in years, but I knew it would happen again one day. I kept hoping it wouldn't be in front of you, or at least not before I could tell you about my epilepsy." He picks up another note and smiles. "How about this one: 'You're the big brother Ryan always wanted.'"

"Well, it's true."

"I don't see Ryan as a younger sibling. I see him as a recalcitrant student who doesn't fully appreciate the value of a thorough education." The sheet flutters into the trash. As my gaze lands on the next note, my blush burns ten times hotter until I'm forced to face the window. "'I want to be your first,'" Vince says without effect.

"Let's skip that one. It's not important."

"But we've already talked about this, Gabby. There's nothing wrong with being someone's third girlfriend. In fact, some may argue it's better—now I know what *not* to do in a relationship."

"That's not the first I was referring to." I'm staring down at the floor now, my whole body threatening spontaneous combustion.

Vince inhales sharply, crumpling the Post-It in his fist. "Oh."

Trapped in awkward silence, dodging each other's gazes, Vince and I let the weight of my admission settle in the tiny sliver of space that separates our bodies. As if sensing this is still too close, Vince shifts a few inches to the left and turns slightly in my direction. "Gabby—"

"We really don't have to talk about this. I was tired when I wrote that, so it doesn't mean anything."

"What about me? Do I mean anything?"

I grab his hand without thinking. "Of course you do. You know that."

"So, let's talk about it." Vince draws a breath and consults the note again. "Here's the thing. My epilepsy affects everything, including how well I can… perform." He clears his throat and darts a glance at the wall.

Once he recovers, he explains, "If there was ever someone I wanted to have that special experience with, it's you. I don't want you to think that I'm depriving you in some way, or that I'm not attracted to you, because you're beautiful. I'm just not sure now's the right time, or when the right time might be."

"I understand." Our fingers are still entwined, so I squeeze his hand. "But just so you know, I'm not with you because I want sex. I'm with you because… I love you. And there are lots of ways to show you that I love you, without you feeling like you have to perform."

Relief highlights Vince's features. When epilepsy robs him of bodily control, I remind myself that the parts I love most about Vince can't be touched by his seizures—things like his ability to see the best in people and his desire to help those around him. He's brilliant, articulate, kind, and tough as old leather. I don't know what happened between him and Diana, but she's given me the greatest gift of all time: the chance to be loved by the boy in the attic.

Vince's lips steal mine, sending lightning bolts of pleasure sweeping over my skin. Downstairs, I hear the front door open. Ryan races into the house hollering like an animal and scampers loudly up the stairs. I barely manage to pry myself off Vince when my brother pops his head into the attic and busts out a grin.

"Vince! You're back!" Ryan exclaims.

Vince rises from the bed, leaving me to clean up the remaining Post-Its. "Sure am. It's the middle of the school year, and I couldn't leave you to fend for yourself."

"Does this mean you're staying?"

"Well, there's plenty of work to be done around here. So, yes."

My goofy little brother fist-pumps the air and retreats to the second floor. He doesn't get excited about much, unless it's video games or candy, but seeing the unadulterated glee in his toothy smile can melt even the coldest hearts, including mine.

Vince addresses me. "I'd better go help your mother."

"And I'd better hit the books."

We fall into our old routine with ease, and the pain of the last three weeks fades away. Vince is back, I finally understand physics, and even the winter chill seems to be taking the hint and leaving us alone. For the first time in months, it feels like everything is going to be okay.

Chapter 17

In the week leading up to the competition, I spend nearly all my free time at the pool. In the water, I'm lean and powerful. Outside of it, I'm a bundle of nerves. Between school, chores, training, and looking after Ryan so mom can take care of herself, I've hardly slept at all. But with Vince picking up the slack, I feel ready for the weekend, even if it means going head-to-head with Melanie in actual competition.

Trisha has been educating herself on Vince's disorder, but still feels uneasy being around him. When I told him this, he suggested spending some time with her on his own, so she could ask her questions and see that people with epilepsy aren't that different from people without. To make matters easier, they plan on hanging out at the pool while I work with Tanya, so I'll be able to keep a close eye on both of them. As if this will quell my anxiety.

"Looks like you doubled up on the distractions today," Tanya says as I hang on to the edge of the pool, trying to catch my breath. She nods at my companions.

I explain, "Trisha saw Vince have a seizure a few weeks ago and it kind of freaked her out. They decided it would be best if they spent some time together, so she can get to know him better."

"At the pool?"

"Well, you *did* say I needed a support network," I remind her, "since Melanie is the chosen one."

Tanya crosses her arms. Nothing exciting ever happens around here, so when someone like Melanie shows up and makes a splash, everyone notices. Her times are consistent, her form is impeccable, and even if you don't know anything about swimming, it's impossible to overlook the girl in the red-hot Speedo who's leaving the rest of us in the dust—or the bubbles, I suppose.

But in friendly competition, when it's just the two of us in an empty pool and Tanya is playing timekeeper at the end of it, Melanie always lags. Tanya claims it's part of her strategy to make me feel like I have a shot at beating her, but Vince genuinely believes I'm the superior swimmer, and it's eating Melanie alive. I guess we'll find out tomorrow, when half the town shows up to watch us race.

"Any last-minute tips?" I ask, climbing out of the water.

"Nothing you don't already know. Get a good night's sleep, pack extras of everything, and try to get here early for warm-ups." Tanya hands me a towel and leads the way to the showers. "Oh, and leave the boyfriend at home. You should only have one thing on your mind tomorrow, and that's swimming."

"Got it," I say, even though I'd never dream of not bringing Vince. Who's going to talk some sense into me when I inevitably get cold feet and want to quit?

Tanya and I go over some final event details. Once that's done, I walk over to where Vince and Trisha are sitting. Trisha is elaborating on her post-graduation plans, how the weather in Jamaica is so much nicer than Canada, and what she plans to eat while she's living and working with her grandmother.

"If you ever come to Jamaica, you have to try fried plantains. Or callaloo. I'll have my grandma make you all kinds of stuff," Trisha promises.

Vince grins and looks up at me. "Well?"

"Yeah, Gabby, how'd it go?" Trisha takes a sip of her mango smoothie.

"You've been here the whole time," I remind them, cocooning myself in a towel.

"True, but we were talking. And you know I can't talk and focus simultaneously," Trisha reminds me.

Vince rummages through my bag and pulls out my water bottle. Taking a seat beside him, I unscrew the cap and take a long drink, trying to visualize the competition and, more importantly, beating Melanie. With her speed, she'll most likely be seeded in one of the centre lanes, where the fastest swimmers have the best advantage. I'll probably end up there, too, though I have yet to meet the other competitors.

"Do you feel ready?" Vince asks.

"I think so. I'm not expecting to win, but I might be able to beat Melanie, if I'm lucky." I tuck my water bottle between my knees and wrap the towel tightly around my shoulders. "Tanya thinks she's holding back so *I'll* hold back. She's never beaten me in a one-on-one race, which is super weird. I mean, it's Melanie Hargrave."

"That's not weird. You have longer arms," Trisha says pointedly.

Vince nods. "She's right. And, when you dive, you enter the water at a steeper angle. Surely, that must have some positive effect on your performance."

"Or maybe," I say, "Tanya's right and Melanie's messing with my head right before a big meet. You guys don't know Melanie like I do. She's ruthless. And she's an extremely sore loser. If I'm her biggest competition, it makes sense that she'd want me to fail."

"Hey, you guys want to get something to eat?" Trisha offers. "We could try that new Thai place by the pet store."

"Not tonight. I can't afford an upset stomach before competition," I explain as I stand up.

Trisha gets to her feet, swings her bag over her shoulder, and tucks her empty plastic cup into the crook of her elbow so she can pull on her mittens. Even though the mud is starting to show through the snow, it'll be another four months (at least) before she feels comfortable enough to leave the house without dressing like she's going on an arctic expedition.

She nudges Vince's arm and smiles. "I'm glad we had a chance to talk."

"Me, too. And if you have any other questions, I'm always available to answer them."

After she leaves, I ask Vince, "Are you okay?"

"No, not really. Did you want to take a shower before we talk about it?"

"Yes." I hand him my water bottle and plant a swift kiss on his cheek that barely escapes Tanya's notice.

Mom's been late picking us up for the past three days and seems on track to continue the streak tonight, so Vince and I wander around the fitness centre while he tells me what's bothering him.

"Big place," he says in response to the indoor running track, its lanes the same crisp blue as those in the pool next door. A handful of runners breeze past us, lost in the heady tonic of music and endorphins. "You wouldn't think a place like this exists so far from the big city."

"I think that's part of the appeal." I lead the way back to the entrance. "So… tomorrow…"

I hear Vince take a breath, like he's preparing to dive deep into the matter rather than skating across it with his typical nonchalance. Part of me knows this is how things will always be in our relationship—uncertain and dictated by his disorder—but I'm still hoping for good news, something I can cling to like a lifesaver. A yes instead of a maybe. But I know it'll never be that simple, even under optimal conditions.

"You know what I'm going to say, don't you?" Vince says flaccidly.

I nod and stare at my shoes. "I know."

"Are you upset?"

"Yes. But I understand why you… don't want to come."

His eyes widen in surprise. "It's not about what I *want* to do, Gabby. Believe me, I want to be here with you more than anything. But if something happens, it's just going to ruin your day. After how hard you've worked, I don't want to be the one who takes that away from you."

We've reached the doors. The wind blows a specter of snow across the parking lot, but I don't see mom's car in any of the spaces.

"I know," I say again, and take his hand. Callouses have formed between his finger joints and I take my time memorizing each one, in case… "It just sucks that you're being excluded. Again."

"I'm not being excluded from anything. It's a choice I'm making—your comfort over mine."

He shouldn't have to make this choice, and certainly not for me, especially after how uncomfortable I made him when he first arrived. There has to be another way. "What if you came for a little while? And if you start to feel overwhelmed, you can step outside. There are going to be lots of heats, so you can take a break in between without missing anything important."

Vince appears to consider this. The meet is supposed to take all afternoon, with competitors broken into groups based on their speeds and judging set to take place after the final heat. Besides, the 50-meter freestyle takes an average, trained swimmer less than thirty seconds from start to finish. What could possibly go wrong in a measly half-minute?

Finally, Vince says, "If it makes you happy, I'll be there." His eyes flicker to the door as a familiar blue car aligns itself with the curb. "There's our ride."

On the drive home, mom and Vince mostly chat about the new subdivision. What used to be arable farmland is now a wide, brown swath of chawed up dirt and rocks. The houses, crammed cheek by jowl along dusty, unfinished streets, range in colour from mouse grey to sunburnt red. Not a tree or shrub or fake flamingo in sight to liven up the scenery. Ironically, this is exactly what my parents despised about living in the city—the inescapable sameness of every day, how the neighbours lived within touching distance of one another, but no one felt close. Vince says Oshawa is like this too, even the nicer parts where his family lives.

When we get home, dad and Ryan are preparing dinner. I'm not particularly hungry, but I force down what I can before escaping to the attic to pack for tomorrow's meet. I pack extras of everything: swimsuits, swim caps, goggles, towels, snacks, and other race-day essentials. Trisha texts me from the Thai food place to give me a review of the service, and I agree to join her next time, when there's no risk of upsetting my already roiling stomach.

The following morning, my appetite is replaced by a dull, throbbing ache in the pit of my stomach. Vince sits in the bathroom with me while I try to decide if I'm going to be sick. After all these months of training, it would be foolish to skip the meet on account of a few frayed nerves, but my body keeps coming up with little ways to torture me. I go back to bed for a couple of hours until I feel the way I should: if not excited for the chance to flaunt my aquatic prowess, then focused on the task at hand, sharp and alert with intention.

By ten o'clock, I drag myself down to the kitchen. The meet is at one, so mom's prepared a bevy of high-protein foods to start my day off strong: scrambled eggs with ketchup, turkey bacon, beans glazed in maple syrup, and toast with peanut butter. The orange slices and strawberry halves are practically glowing with freshness. The breakfast of champions.

"Good morning!" mom says a little too enthusiastically. "Do you like the breakfast?"

"I'll let you know what my stomach thinks in half an hour." I give up trying to slice the bacon with my knife and, instead, lift the rubbery strip of meat straight into my mouth with my fingers.

Mom places something beside me: a bracelet.

"What's this?" I ask, picking up the gold bangle and examining its incomplete circular shape. The part that goes around my wrist is shiny and cold, and its ends culminate in a pair of spherical knobs separated by a narrow gap.

Mom explains, "It's a balance bracelet. It helps to keep your chakras in alignment."

I lower the bangle. "Mom, you don't even know what a chakra *is*."

"Maybe not, but I know my daughter, and she is going to win." Mom kisses my head and rubs my shoulders with velvet hands.

I grudgingly consent to wearing the bracelet with questionable spiritual benefits. (I can always toss it in my swim bag if it starts to weigh me, or my chakras, down.) I've nearly finished eating when Vince walks in, pours himself a coffee, and sits down beside me. He's wearing a bracelet too, but his has nothing to do with balance, chakras, or beating Melanie Hargrave.

I flip the little metal tag over, which has his name (Vincent McCarthy) on one side and his condition and medication (Epilepsy, Phenobarbital) on the other. "When did you start wearing this?" I ask.

Vince avoids my gaze. "A few weeks ago. You must not have seen it under my sleeves."

"Vince." When our eyes meet, I say, "Please don't lie to me. Not today."

"You're right. I'm sorry. I brought it with me when I moved to town, only I didn't wear it because I was more concerned with impressing you than protecting myself."

"Well, that was stupid."

"I know." Vince slurps some coffee. "How are you feeling now?"

"Not horrible, not great. The breakfast is helping though."

It's now 10:30, late for anything farm-related, but Vince seems to be in a hurry and blitzes off on a new mission, leaving me to finish breakfast alone.

Food is not the only thing I'm forced to swallow today: ever since beating Melanie in training, my ego has become problematically large. She's not going to be my only competition though, and a lot of the people who enter the Spring Swim-a-thon have more years of training, better coaches, and a stronger drive to win. I go over my technique in my head while I shower, dress, and round up the last of my possessions. By noon, the truck is packed and the five of us head to the pool.

What's old is new again as we walk through the doors and into the bustling lobby. I instinctively grab Vince's hand as we navigate the mob. There's so much noise. Endless commotion. Vince's fingers cut into mine, but he presses forward. Soon, the crowd thins out and we emerge poolside, where a handful of swimmers are warming up. Their families are gathered in the stands, armed with coffees and cameras. Closer to the water, a news crew is setting up equipment, testing microphones, and going over their notes. An actual news crew, from an actual TV news station, is here at the Spring Swim-a-thon, ready to capture the action as it happens.

My stomach twists. I turn to Vince and say, "I can't do this."

"Why not?"

"Because I just can't. It's too much pressure."

His expression softens. "Trust me, you can. And I'm going to be here the whole time."

Mom, dad, and Ryan have finally managed to escape the human maze and walk straight over to us, carried by the waves of anticipation.

"Whoa!" Ryan points to the reporters assembled near the judges' tables. "TV people!"

"I think they're covering the meet to try and lure city folks into town, to fill all the new houses being built," mom says. "At least, that's what Donna Miller told me."

Donna Miller owns the property next door, and since her husband serves on the town council, she knows what's happening long before the rest of us do. "I hope their cameras are waterproof," I say halfheartedly.

"We're going to find some seats," dad tells me, though he looks at Vince while he speaks. No doubt the two of them have already pinned down the most practical place to sit when your party includes a kid, a guy with epilepsy, and a mother who drinks excessive quantities of tea.

Vince nods, telling my father, "I'll be right there, once I finish giving Gabby a pep talk."

"Feel free to skip the pep talk. I already know what you're going to say," I tell him.

"No, you don't. I know you're scared. I'm scared, too. And if you wanted to quit, I'd understand." Vince holds my gaze. "The first time I drove you to the pool, you asked me if I had a diving board story. I do. When I was a kid, I loved theatre. I even starred in a couple of plays, including *Peter Pan* and *Romeo and Juliet*. I had a seizure on stage while playing Romeo, and an audience of twelve-year-olds is the toughest, cruelest crowd there is." More families trickle in. Vince adds, "I quit theatre a week later. Epilepsy felt like a bigger part of my life and I let it blind me to what actually mattered. That's the difference between you and me, Gabby: I'm a quitter, you aren't. And even if you don't win, you're still a champion in my books." Vince cups his hands around my face and studies me with his beautiful eyes. "Remember: just breathe."

After Vince joins my family in the stands, I haul my gear into the changeroom. A row of cubicles separated by powder blue walls stretches along the back of the room. The floors are so shiny, I can view my reflection in the tiles. Across from the change stalls, a long, white counter provides ample space to indulge one's vanity. Placing my bag on the counter, I unzip one of the compartments and pull out a hairbrush, some bobby pins, and a tube of waterproof mascara for after the meet, when mom goes on her picture-taking rampage. And, okay, for Vince.

A stall door opens in the distance. Someone slams their bag down beside mine, leans toward the mirror, and laments, "Of course I'd have a breakout the day I'm going to be on TV."

You guessed it: the owner of the oily skin is Melanie. I'm unspeakably glad everyone is going to be looking at her today, all shiny and blistered with excess hormones.

She withdraws from the mirror and ferrets around in her bag. "I wish I had skin like yours."

"Aw. Thanks."

"I mean you look like a corpse. Dead people don't get acne." Then Melanie starts dabbing foundation on the clusters until they disappear.

I smile contritely. She's not wrong about my complexion: dad's pale, Irish skin is in my genes. But so are mom's long arms.

"Looks like someone had a few too many deep-fried Oreos at the fair," I mutter.

Melanie shoots me a warning glance in the mirror. She knows I'm only having a bit of fun at her expense. Getting into the competitive mood, as it were.

Her eyes drift back to her face, half-covered by liquid skin. "I saw your boyfriend in the crowd."

"And?"

She sponges makeup into the creases of her nose. "It's a big crowd. Lots of loud noises and bright lights."

I stare at her, my mouth dry as a stone, wondering how she could possibly know about Vince's epilepsy. And then I remember: that week Trisha and I weren't talking, she was chumming it up with Elaine, our resident mad scientist. Elaine and Melanie are best friends—and best friends tell each other everything.

Melanie's finally evened out her skin tone. External beauty to hide the ugliness within. "Well, I should go warm up." She pulls her swim cap out of her bag, rolls it over her head, and hangs her goggles on her wrist.

I follow her out of the changeroom and down the hallway leading to the pool. My blood is boiling. A little voice at the back of my mind that sounds an awful lot like Vince's urges me to take the high road and pretend Melanie doesn't exist. *Breathe*, he'd tell me.

"Hey, Melanie."

She turns around. Beyond the hallway, Tanya does the same.

I look at my opponent again. "Good luck out there."

Melanie smiles inscrutably and proceeds to the warmup area to stake out her territory closest to the camera crew.

Once I'm in my swimsuit, my mind instantly feels calmer. I'm good at this. The water is my refuge. I smooth down my silicone cap and face myself one last time, feeding my starving confidence micro-doses of positive affirmation. *I am strong. I am fast. I am amazing.*

The stands are bursting with spectators. Some of the faces are familiar, but most belong to people I've never met, out-of-towners intent on checking out the local sports scene. Mom, dad, Ryan, and Vince are seated near the stairs halfway up the stands. As I look over at him, Vince smiles and flashes a discreet thumbs-up gesture—either *good luck* or *I'm okay*. I decide it's both, and make my way over to Tanya for some final words of wisdom.

"Ready?" She takes in my blue-and-black swim suit, which hugs my body like Saran wrap.

"I think so." I glimpse the pool, smell the chlorine wafting off the turquoise surface. The judges are congregating next to lane one, where they'll have front row seats to every little mistake.

Tanya shows me her paperwork. "Look, you're in the third heat, lane five, for the 50-meter freestyle."

"Lane five? Are you sure?"

"That's what the heat sheet says." She tucks the clipboard under her arm. "Melanie's times are similar to yours, but she's not the only one you have to watch out for. Isobel Hutchison was seeded into lane four of the third heat of the 50-meter. That makes her your biggest competition right now."

"Yeah, but Isobel doesn't have a personal vendetta against me," I point out.

"Remember what I said about having a bag of rocks?" When I nod, Tanya says, "Everyone has a bag of rocks. Some people's bags are filled with insecurity and poor sportsmanship. Yours is filled with needless distractions. Let go of the bag, and you might just win this thing." She squeezes my shoulder. "Make me proud out there, Gabby," she says, and leaves me alone so I can untie whatever weighs me down.

After about twenty minutes, the first heat assembles. Eight swimmers mount their respective blocks, give their goggles one last tap for fit, and hunch into the starting position. A hush falls over the arena as we wait for the pop of the pistol. Then it's just noise as they dive into the water. The swimmers in lanes three, four, and five take the lead, but it's a close race. At the opposite end of the pool, their coaches are waiting. Tense. After about thirty-three seconds, the swimmer in lane five reaches the finish line and beats her fist against the air. I don't know her personally, but she's just earned herself a spot in the finals. As the rest of the swimmers latch on to the edge, times are recorded, and the first heat makes its exit from the pool.

I glance over at Vince. He's talking to mom as if they're at home in the kitchen, making dinner instead of watching me swim. As his eyes return to my face, I breathe a sigh of relief. Vince looks fine. And if he's fine, then I am, too.

By the time the third heat is called, every cell in my body is tingling. I shake my hands, loosen up my shoulders, and pull down my goggles. I feel the block's rough cover under my feet, giving me stability where my knees fail. Noisy breaths fill the silence on both sides. Leaning forward, I grasp the edge of the block and prepare to dive.

When the pistol fires, all eight of us enter the water. The hum of human voices vanishes as I glide beneath the surface. I keep my face down and my head straight, using the black lines on the floor to approximate my location in the pool. As I come up for my first breath, the fervor rushes in to fill my ears: kids screaming, parents cheering, the endless crashing of water from all sides. I fill my lungs and pull my face underwater again. Bubbles stream from my feet as I work my legs up and down, not too fast, not too slow. I picture Paulette Klein, the Olympic swimmer who serves as my inspiration, and feel a lightness in my body that can only be described as letting go. Say goodbye to the rocks. And come in first place.

Tanya is waiting for me at the end of the lane like always, towel at the ready. She tells me my time: 33.872 seconds. Her mouth keeps moving, but I only hear the last thing she says, which is that I'll be swimming in the finals alongside the fastest swimmers from heats one and two. And Isobel Hutchison won't be joining us.

There's a short break as the fourth heat readies itself to race, and I take the opportunity to check in with my family.

Vince trots down the metal stairs. Mom is right behind him, but dad and Ryan decide to hang back, presumably to save their seats. I throw myself into Vince's arms, reveling in the warmth of his embrace and the just-showered smell of his skin. His MedicAlert bracelet digs into my back.

He pulls away, grinning. "You were amazing."

Mom reaches in for her own hug, which is slightly softer and warmer than Vince's, but a little too tight. "Ah-may-zing!" she sings, drawing out each syllable.

I tell them, "I couldn't have done it without all of you. And Tanya. And Paulette Klein."

"Who's Paulette?" Vince asks.

Mom replies, "Gabby's role model. She swims for Team Canada."

"Ah." Glancing over his shoulder at Ryan, Vince muses, "I suppose it's good to have role models, no matter who you are."

"Anyway, we should get back to our seats. You"—Mom squishes my cheeks between her palms like I'm a ball of cookie dough waiting to be rolled out and cut into pretty shapes—"Stay focused. Be the water."

"Be the water," I repeat.

The remaining heats in the 50-meter freestyle soon reveal their finals qualifiers. One girl, Molly Brown, sets an unbeatable record of 29.133 seconds. She's not particularly tall, but she packs the same lethal punch as a bullet, blasting from one end of the pool to the other so fast that even the judges can't believe what they're seeing. The look they pass around as they record her time for future seeding tells me they think there's been some kind of mistake. Or that she's doping. But talk of performance-enhancing drugs won't lure middle-class families to a town with only one Tim Hortons, so her unbelievable time goes without question.

I sneak off to the bathroom during the last heat for this event and miss hearing the fastest time. But when I get back poolside, one section of the crowd is going berserk. That's when I see them, leaping up and down in the top row, belting out a name I know all too well. It's Elaine and Casey, cheering Melanie on. When Casey sees me, he has the audacity to wave.

Melanie struts over to me. Some of her makeup's washed off, but she's glowing like a candle. The judges adore her. From way up in the crowd, Casey calls out, "Melanie, I love you!" at full, hand-cupped volume, and she responds by blowing him a kiss that has the TV crew salivating.

"Isn't he incredible?" Melanie asks, tacking on a wink for good measure. "We'll take our nominations for prom king and queen now, please."

"You guys won't make it to March break, much less senior year," I say.

"That's what you think." I roll my eyes. "Good swimming, by the way. A little sloppy, but hey, we can't all be perfect."

"Yeah, that's true. Maybe once your breakout's over, you won't have so much crap weighing you down."

Melanie snarls and brushes past me, to dry off and cool down with the others.

As the afternoon wears on, a small thorn of dread begins pinching me from the inside. Melanie and I, together in the finals, isn't what I had in mind all those months ago when I agreed to sign up for the meet. I expected she'd be too busy with her other sports to take the competition seriously, or that I'd be pitifully slow and not even crop up on her radar. But life is funny like that: sometimes, the obstacles find you.

I swim the 100-meter freestyle in two minutes, three-point-eight-nine seconds. Fourth place. Molly crushes everyone with her flashy one minute, fifty-five seconds. Skepticism works its way through the judges' table, but again, they find no cause to suspend her. What's strange is that Melanie, who's also in this event, doesn't consider Molly a serious threat. I conclude that her indifference has two possible explanations: either she knows with absolute certainty that Molly's success is steeped in banned substances, or they're conspiring with each other to make me quit. Besides, if I truly am *ah-may-zing*, why wouldn't Molly and Melanie want me gone?

Breathe, I tell myself over and over. Be the water and flush them out.

By four o'clock, the final event in the 50-meter freestyle is afoot. The crowd is growing restless; some people have already left, along with a number of competitors who didn't make the cut. The remaining eyes are on the pool, which looks even bigger and brighter now that the sun's all but gone, leaving the overhead lights the sole source of illumination. Up in the stands, Ryan is pestering mom for one of her purse candies. Vince, on her opposite side, is watching me. He bobs his chin in a curt nod of encouragement. His fingers are worrying his MedicAlert bracelet, sending up red flags in my mind. When we first learned about his epilepsy, he told me he can usually anticipate when a seizure is imminent. He describes it as feeling "out of sorts," or becoming irritated by things that would normally escape his notice. He's been here for hours, not eating, surrounded by a sea of triggers, and for what? To watch me splash around in a giant bathtub?

Tanya walks over to me. "You're almost up."

"I know." My thoughts scatter, breaking up my pre-race concentration. I should check on Vince, make sure he's okay, and get him someplace safe if he's feeling in any way unusual.

As if reading my mind, Tanya warns, "If you go up there—"

"I just need to check on my boyfriend. That's all."

"That's not happening. I won't allow it."

"Tanya—"

"Gabby, listen to me. We had an agreement. If you want to have a swimming career, then you have to make every race count. There will always be another boyfriend, but opportunities come once or never at all." She adds, "There are talent scouts in this crowd. Swimming coaches from universities all across Ontario. They came to look for people like you, and if you run off now, they'll know you're not serious enough to be on their teams. Is that what you want?"

I set my jaw, knowing she's right and that Vince will have to wait. As Tanya takes my towel and walks me to the starting block, the echoes of our conversation from a few weeks ago drift back to me. These are the better coaches she alluded to, the bright future I must be bold enough to grab. I take my place in front of lane five. Molly swaggers up to lane four, and beside her, in lane three, is Melanie.

Tanya whispers behind me, "Breathe." I do.

The goggles are as tight as ever. My swimsuit, suffocating. I smooth down the cap and shake my arms. Melanie glances over at me, looking right past Molly like she doesn't exist, and because I know who's in the crowd now, I mouth, "Good luck." My kindness isn't returned.

A voice in the speakers says, "Racers ready." All eight of us lean forward with knees slightly bent, ready to take the plunge.

Silence.

Pop. The pistol fires. Water envelopes my body, forming a protective layer between me and the outside world. Then, like being born, I emerge and take my first breath. I reach my arms as far as they physically go, until my shoulders burn from the strain. Left, right, left, right. Molly has a slight lead. No surprises there. I go facedown again, see the halfway point zip past me, and dare to imagine what the future holds. *Breathe.* I draw in air and a brief glimpse at the stands, where my family is on their feet. Ryan is bouncing with excitement. I only catch Vince's hair before I dip beneath the surface again.

The lines on the bottom of the pool tell me I'm close to finishing. I dig down deep and find an extra dose of confidence, enough for a quick burst of speed near the end. My fingers jam against the wall almost unexpectedly.

I lift my face out of the water, remove my goggles. Look back and see Molly and Melanie catching up.

My time on the leader board: 29.085.

As I'm helped out of the water, mom pushes through the throng of coaches and swimmers to reach me. She squeals, "Gabby!" and reels me into her arms for a hug.

I don't really believe I've won, not until dad, Ryan, and Vince walk over and congratulate me. Even then, I wait for the punchline. Instead, I get Vince's soft mouth against my lips, rousing me from my stupor.

He presses his forehead against mine and whispers, *Amazing.*

"Gabby." Tanya's voice breaks the spell. Next to her, a man in a suit awaits an introduction.

As I walk over to them, promising my family I'll be right back, my coach says, "Gabby, I'd like you to meet Leo Walsh. He coaches the swimming team at the University of Toronto."

Leo smiles and says, "I couldn't help but take notice of your track record. Tanya tells me you've been swimming since you were three. Is that correct?"

"Yes, sir."

"In that case, I'd like to talk to you about your academic future and what kinds of scholarships are available to promising young athletes such as yourself." He motions to one of the benches, where we can expect to find a bit of privacy.

Leo gives me a rundown of life at U of T. It's nestled in the heart of our province's capital, an almost unfathomable distance from our family-run dairy farm. He's come prepared with brochures, program guides, and business cards, all of which he gives me to look over once I'm at home.

After Leo and I finish talking, Tanya introduces me to a few more coaches. Mom dutifully stockpiles the information packages from Western, Waterloo, and Queen's. It's tough to tell which of us is more excited. Six months ago, I wasn't even thinking about life after high school. Now, several institutions are vying for my application. Dad tells me not to worry about the cost; they'll find a way to afford the future Tanya promised.

Before the day is over, Tanya shepherds me over to the podium to accept my medal. Gold. From up on the platform, I look across the pool, see Vince sitting with my family, and mouth, "Thank you." For being here, for pushing me, for reminding me that we are limitless. He just smiles. After all, he knew what I was capable of all along.

Chapter 18

"New guy at twelve o'clock," Trisha announces.

I swivel my head around and let my gaze rest on a face six lockers and one classroom door away. He's wearing brand-spanking-new Timberland boots, dark jeans, and a Canada Goose jacket. "We have to stop calling him 'new guy,'" I say as I turn back to Trisha.

"I can't help it. If I say his name, I break out in hives."

"And what is his name?" Trisha ignores me, so I ask again, "Name?"

She sighs. Her eyes drift over my head and latch on to Mr. Money again. "His name's Chas Lewis. He's in my math class."

"Look at that—no allergic reaction."

"Then why does my throat swell up whenever he's around?" Trisha's eyes widen. "Oh, god. He's looking over here."

In all the years we've been friends, I've never seen Trisha get so flustered over a guy. Her parents doubled down on the no-dating-until-you're-thirty rule when Caitlin became pregnant at sixteen, and having a squalling baby in the house solidified Trisha's revulsion toward men. But there's a first time for everything, and I've been waiting eons for the chance to double-date with my best friend.

"If he's new, he probably doesn't have any friends," I say, reveling in the terror that flickers in Trisha's brown eyes. "Wouldn't it be nice if we were the first?"

"You know, I think I saw him eating lunch with Brian Legault."

"Brian's a loser. Chas deserves better." I take her hand and lead her into uncharted territory. If Vince were here, he'd march right over and introduce himself, and that would be that. Chas would be the most popular kid in school in no time.

As Chas looks up from his phone and sees us walking toward him, Trisha practically wheezes. I think the bones in my hand might be broken.

"Gabby—"

"Breathe," I urge her. Chas is standing directly in front of us now, so I smile. "Hey. You're new here, right?"

"Um." He looks around like I might be talking to someone else. "Yeah."

"I'm Gabby, and this is my best friend, Trisha. She says you two are in the same math class."

A hint of a smile traces his mouth. "Yeah. You let me copy your notes from last week." He's speaking directly to Trisha now, in a voice that's deeper than Vince's but no less kind. "That was cool of you. Especially since it's the middle of the school year."

"It's nothing." Trisha looks down at the floor.

Well, this is going better than I'd hoped. I pretend to check my phone, then announce with false urgency, "I'm super late for study group. But maybe you should have lunch with us sometime."

"Cool," Chas says, once again looking at Trisha, "if that's okay with you."

"Super okay with me."

I take my leave, mouthing "Text me" to Trisha as I head down the hall to my next class. When I'm a safe distance away, I peek over my shoulder and find her laughing at something he said. If Vince and I, who couldn't be more different, could end up together and be happy, I'm convinced anything is possible.

*

Newton's third law of physics states that for every action, there is an equal, and opposite, reaction. Over the next several days, I get to witness these actions and reactions in real time, and feel their energies reverberating through every corner of my life.

"Ugh, look at them," Elaine says, directing our eyes toward a table across the cafeteria. Trisha has been eating lunch with Chas every day this week, then calling me in the evenings to share the juicy details. It's driving Elaine insane, seeing what real chemistry looks like. "So much for smashing the patriarchy. I mean, he's not even that cute."

"You're only saying that because you can't have him," I reply.

Elaine feigns disbelief. She takes an unreasonably long drink of her Perrier water and says, "Give it time, kitten. Once he sees she's not ready for a relationship, he'll drop her faster than a new Taylor Swift song."

I shake my head. Trisha and Chas are poring over a math textbook, sitting shoulder to shoulder to read the equations. Even Elaine can't get between that, no matter how much she wants to.

I reach for my backpack and swing it onto my shoulder. Ever since Leo Walsh came into our lives, mom and I have been charting my post-secondary career and making sure I register for all the right classes next year. Unfortunately, that means improving my grades *now*, right at the peak of Trisha and Chas's infatuation for each other. It wasn't the sacrifice I was expecting, but it's one I'm prepared to make if it means having the chance to live in Toronto and train with the best.

As I walk past their table, Trisha leaps out of her seat and threads her arm through mine. Chas looks too vulnerable sitting there alone, but Elaine shows some restraint, for once, and goes back to her overpriced fizzy water.

"Sick of him already, huh?" I say.

"Not even close." As soon as we're outside the cafeteria, she pulls me to the side and squeaks, "He asked me to the spring formal."

My eyes widen. "Wait, really? But you've only known him for five minutes."

"So? When someone asks you to spring formal, you say yes. That's the rule." Trisha's gaze flickers back to the overcrowded lunch room, presumably to make sure Elaine hasn't made a move on her man. "I need your help."

"With what?"

"Everything! I've never gone to a dance before. Not with a guy, at least." Just like that, Trisha is a breathless, flustered mess. She flutters her hands a few times as if it will help to dispel some of her apprehension, then whines, "I have nothing to wear! Nothing that sparkles! I need you to bedazzle me, Gabby."

"Okay, but not right now. I have to meet with my bio teacher to go over my latest test. But, I promise, we'll go shopping this weekend."

"That's not soon enough. I require your services *now*."

"Why?" As Trisha's smile fades, I begin to understand her urgency. I reach for her fingers, enfolding them in the protection of my own. "He's not going to lose interest, Trish. Chas likes you for *you*, just like Vince loves me for me."

"Are you sure? Like you said, it's only been five minutes."

"I'm positive." As we hug, I whisper, "Sparkles or no sparkles, he can't take his eyes off you."

Trisha and I let go. Her eyes narrow on Elaine again, but Chas, having grown bored of eating lunch alone, closes the textbook and takes his leave. He swaggers across the cafeteria, turning a few heads with his pricey wardrobe, then steps through the doors and walks toward us.

She tells him, "Gabby and I were just discussing the spring formal." His smile grows.

"Okay, I seriously have to go," I say, giving Trisha's hand a quick squeeze as I step around her. "I'll call you tonight."

"Promise?"

I turn back to Trisha with a smirk. "Of course. We're a team, aren't we?"

*

Spring arrives with a flourish. Almost overnight, the flowers in mom's garden go from unsightly brown stalks to lush green leaves ornamented with colourful blooms. The tulips awaken first, sprinkling the garden with pops of lemon yellow and pastel pink. As the snow recedes, giving the grass a chance to breathe and the dandelions room to grow, Vince and dad spend almost all their time with the cows. Most of the calves are born in the field, with little to no human interference. The calves are sorted by sex, with the males being sent away and the females kept as replacements for the cows approaching retirement. It's a grim reminder that a working farm is no place to form emotional attachments. Vince's acceptance letter from American University drives the point home.

"We should celebrate," mom says. She disappears to the basement for a few minutes. When she returns, holding a tub of Death by Chocolate ice cream that's been buried in our chest freezer, Ryan promptly loses his mind.

"All right! Ice cream for dinner!" my brother enthuses.

"Ice cream for *after* dinner," mom says. Vince has nearly finished setting the table, leaving me to arrange the contents of the breadbasket.

Ryan scowls. "We never do anything fun."

"That's because you ruin every fun thing we do," I tell him, transferring the dinner rolls to the table. "Family movie night, family board game night, family dinner—"

"That's a lie," Ryan argues. "I'm fun, *you're* boring. That's why dad hired Vince—so you'd be less boring."

Vince raises his hands. "I'm not getting in the middle of this one."

We take our usual places at the table. Soon, dad walks in from the barn and joins us. He's already started looking for someone to replace Vince, since I'll be working at the pool this summer to earn money for university. But so far, no takers.

Dad starts the conversation by saying, "So, I hear congratulations are in order." He looks at Vince and smiles. "How soon do you plan on leaving?"

"Eager to have me gone, Mr. O'Connor?" Vince jokes. "I can leave tomorrow, if it makes you happy."

"No, no, I just want to make sure you have everything you need before you tackle the next chapter of your life. Sounds like it'll be an exciting one."

Vince pierces one of the potatoes with his fork. We haven't talked much about his leaving, something I habitually blame on my hectic training schedule and excess quantities of homework. Everyone knows long-distance relationships never work out, especially at our age.

"By the way, Gabby," mom says, "Trisha called for you. I don't know why she called the house, but it sounded important."

"Probably something to do with the spring formal. I promised I'd bedazzle her."

"Why does she need you to bedazzle her?" dad asks. "Doesn't she have an older sister she can ask for fashion advice?"

"She does, but Caitlin works a lot and has a kid. And I guess it's partly my fault that Trisha is going to the spring formal to begin with. I mean, if I hadn't introduced her to Chas, none of this would've happened."

"Are you going to spring formal, Gabby?" Ryan asks.

I chew my latest mouthful until it's nothing more than a tasteless pulp. Who would I even go with? Vince? He'd surely say no on account of his epilepsy, although he'd be equally quick to encourage me to go and have a good time on his behalf. As if.

Vince says, "I think Gabby should go. We all deserve a break now and then, right?"

"I agree. Besides, Trisha might need you," mom adds sensibly.

I finally swallow. "I'm still thinking about it. This semester's pretty brutal, and I need to keep my grades up for next year."

No one argues with this. After dinner, I help mom wash and put away the dishes before heading upstairs to tackle the mountain of biology homework. Before long, the soft tread of footsteps enters my space. Vince crosses the attic in long, sweeping strides, but rather than going straight to his half, he leans on the back of my chair and asks, "What are you learning?"

"How DNA replicates." I look up from the pages of my textbook, where helicase is unraveling a strand of genetic material, one nucleotide base pair at a time. "Shouldn't you be helping dad?"

"Are you trying to get rid of me, too?" He smirks and sinks down on my bed.

Setting down my pen, I turn sideways in my chair until Vince and I are facing each other. "I'll go to the spring formal... under one condition," I say.

"What's that?"

"If you come with me. Technically, there's no rule that says we can't bring guests from outside of school..." As he opens his mouth to protest, I say, "I know you're going to say no. And I understand why. But if I had a choice, I'd choose you."

"I'm flattered. But I don't want you to miss out on a good time because of me." Vince stares down at his hands. "My sister, Natalie, lost out on a chance to be the lead singer in her high school's musical because I had a bad seizure and broke my wrist. Despite what she says, I know she hasn't forgiven me for stealing the attention away from her. That's why I want you to go to the spring formal with Trisha and have a good time."

"Or else what—you'll pack your bags and go to Washington tomorrow?"

"If that's what it takes."

I shake my head. Men—always leaving when you need them most. "Come with me. Please."

He collects my hands in his, lightly presses his lips to mine in what I take to be an apology, and rises from the bed. But I don't let go.

"Gabby, I'm not going to change my mind," he says.

"Then maybe we can compromise."

Vince's eyes narrow on me. He's sturdy but unresisting as I reach for his shirt and close the space that separates us. His mouth softens under my lips. His muscles, which now feel more like Jayden's, tense under my touch.

"I don't think this is a good idea," he whispers. I wait for him to pull away, but his hands remain on my waist—right where they'd be if he agreed to go to the spring formal with me, and if there was music and we were dancing.

"Why not?"

"Because you're still in high school. You have an amazingly bright future ahead of you, and I won't be responsible for taking it away." Vince's hands migrate to my face. Even the webbing of his fingers feels more durable, the pads of his thumbs thicker than when he first arrived. "I can wait."

"I can't."

"You have to. There's no fast-forward button." He continues, "When I go to Washington, everything is going to change. And that scares me."

"It scares me, too."

"I don't know what things between us are going to be like in a year, but I know I don't want to rush something so special, especially with you." Vince drops his hands. They don't even stop at my waist this time, and I try not to look as disappointed as I feel.

Mom calls up the stairs to inform Vince of evening chores. The violet tint of dusk seeps into the air and trees outside as he answers back, making the floors and rafters tremble with the echo of his voice. He's right—now is not the time for us to be getting closer. If we go to the spring formal together, it will cement the idea that we're a couple and that our future is set in stone. But we aren't and it isn't. At the end of the day, I'm just the farmer's daughter and he's just the hired hand.

Before he leaves, Vince leans toward me and lands a swift, featherlight kiss on my lips. It's superficial, like dipping your fingers into a pool to test the warmth of the water. And then he's gone.

Chapter 19

The lineup to purchase tickets for the spring formal wends through the halls and around the cafeteria. The dance is only for juniors, since the seniors have prom at the end of the year, plus a chance to flee this place at graduation. My promise to bedazzle Trisha has so far gone unfulfilled, what with work picking up on the farm and Vince preparing to go to Washington. I'm still not one hundred percent sold on the idea of attending spring formal solo, but Vince is adamant that I'll enjoy myself. Who am I to doubt him, when his optimism has gotten me this far?

"I heard Elaine's going with Ethan," Trisha says mid-text. "It's probably just a rumour, but can you imagine?"

"If he does make an appearance, you can bet it'll be in a body bag," I reply.

She smirks, scanning the faces in our vicinity to gauge who else we might expect to see at the dance. "What about Vince?"

"What do you mean?"

"You know," Trisha intones, nudging me with her elbow, "if he dresses as well as he talks, then you're in for a *treat*."

My face falls. The line shuffles forward a couple of steps, then stops again. "He's not coming," I deadpan, leaning my head against the locker.

Trisha furrows her brows. "What do you mean, he's not coming? It's Vince. He comes to all of your big events."

"Not all."

The people ahead of us creep forward. "Did he say why he's not coming?"

I don't answer her. Last night's conversation in the attic has been playing on repeat in my mind all day. At first, it seemed like Vince's reservations stemmed from him not wanting his epilepsy to interfere with what should be a night of fun and frivolity. But then I realized his epilepsy is a cover for a lot of other things—namely his fear of getting close to people. We've nearly reached the ticket table, but I can't muster the same level of excitement that keeps Trisha bouncing on the balls of her feet, thrilled by the prospect of being transformed into a human chandelier.

Chas rounds the corner and makes a beeline for where we're standing. When he gets closer, he pulls a twenty out of his pocket and slots himself between me and Trisha, claiming the space beside her as his own.

"Two more weeks," he announces, slinging an arm around her shoulder. His eyes lock on my face with a puzzled expression. "Where's your date?"

"What date?" I drawl, infusing my voice with maximum sarcasm. "Oh, that's right—I don't have one."

"Then why are you in line?"

I motion to Trisha, who's stuck on Chas like a wad of freshly-chewed gum. "Same reason you are. Vince is making me buy a ticket so I don't miss out on any fun, but I'll probably spend the whole night in the corner by myself."

"You won't be by yourself—we'll be there, too," Trisha cuts in, reaching around Chas to jab my arm with her wallet.

I indulge her with a smile, even though I know it'll feel like hanging out with a couple of houseplants for how little they'll notice me. Once we reach the table, Trisha and Chas each part with a twenty-dollar bill and receive a yellow paper ticket authenticated with the school's official stamp. Go Badgers.

"We'll save you a spot," Trisha tells me, and she and Chas head to the cafeteria. There's no question they're a couple, and that neither of them is planning to go to Washington anytime soon.

I step forward. Sarah Egerton and Kayleigh Price stop gossiping long enough to give me matching smiles.

"Two tickets?" Kayleigh, the blonde one, lilts. Her hand hovers expectantly over the stack of little yellow slips.

I force myself to smile back. "Just one." I hand over the money.

Sarah stuffs the bill into the metal box without comment. Kayleigh picks up a ticket, rubs the corner of it between her thumb and forefinger to ensure there's only one, and hands it to me.

"Have fun," they crow as I walk away. The next couple in line marches up to their table, pays for their tickets, and starts the gossip cycle up again.

This won't be so bad, I tell myself as I enter the cafeteria. It's just one night, after all. Vince left us for three weeks during the winter, and I didn't fall apart then. Chas and Trisha are sitting at their usual table, and she's whispering something in his ear, as if anyone will hear them over their full mouths and empty chatter. When she spots me, Trisha waves her hand and I swallow the bitter taste of jealousy.

"Are you going to be okay?" she asks as I sit down across from them and pull a bottle of Pepsi out of my backpack.

"Of course. It's just a dance."

Trisha shakes her head. "Once a terrible liar, always a terrible liar."

They unpack their lunches and start eating. I seem to have misplaced my appetite, so I sip my drink and stare at my phone. When the bell rings, I leap out of my chair and head straight for the doors, then down the hall and out to the school yard, where the air is clean and I can finally breathe.

Chapter 20

Trisha is dazzling. Even without my intervention, she's managed to capture every beam radiating from the string of globe lights hung around the banquet hall. Sheathed in a daffodil-yellow A-line dress with a flared skirt and sequined bodice, she takes Chas by the hand and whisks him to the centre of the dance floor as the music shifts from spiky electropop to a slow, sensual ballad. Chas is wearing a creamy white tuxedo with an actual daffodil tucked in his lapel, and his arms are tight around Trisha's waist. Nothing like a high school dance to make the extremely intimate act of falling in love feel like the most must-see event of the year. All the same, I can't take my eyes off of them. They're oozing happiness while I'm sitting by myself at a table in the corner, compulsively smoothing down my dress even though I know no one will ask me to dance. Even Casey, who's been orbiting the room all night, barely acknowledges me between sips of Coke. It would be a perfect night, if not for one glaring omission: Vince.

"You're not dancing?"

I look up from the glitzy blue material of my dress to see Carla clopping across the wooden floor in sleek black heels. I guess riding horses has given her superb balance and natural finesse. The glass of sparkling water she carries is practically undisturbed.

"I'm not much of a dancer," I admit as she takes a seat in Trisha's vacated chair and sets her drink on the table.

"Me neither. Although I think I may have a secret admirer," she adds conspiratorially.

"Who?"

Carla nods at a silhouette across the room. Brian perks up instantly. His slacks end in puddles around his ankles and he's taken the liberty of loosening his tie. As disheveled as he is, this look is a big step up from his usual just-rolled-out-of-bed aesthetic. He's even combed down his jet-black hair, which ordinarily resembles a sea urchin on dry land.

Brian leans forward in his chair like he wants to approach us, then pretends to be more interested in his phone.

I grimace. "Not for all the money in the world," I say in answer to an unspoken question. "You?"

Carla shrugs and takes a sip of her drink. "I could do better, but I could also do worse. And at least I wouldn't be sitting at a table by myself."

We sit in companionable silence, watching the other couples sway and twirl across the dance floor. Elaine has decided to upstage us all in a hot pink ball gown and matching shoes. Ethan is with her (alive, thankfully) and I can't tell if he's being held against his will or if he's finally realized that the phrase "Hold your friends close and your enemies closer" was a reference to Elaine. But it's the spring formal, and there's no telling what kind of magic will bloom tonight.

Carla stands up, chugs the last of her fizzy water, and announces, "Wish me luck."

"With what?" I ask.

She turns halfway toward Brian, who once again comes to life at the possibility of being noticed. His hand reaches for his tie and slides the knot up to his throat. Progress.

"I want to dance with someone other than my horse," Carla says, blushing a little as the words leave her mouth. "Hopefully, Zeus won't be too jealous."

It's hard to believe anyone would be jealous of Brian, but instead, I smile and say, "Good luck." She treks across the room, her black dress swishing back and forth with each step. She and Brian exchange what I imagine are the usual pleasantries, before Brian rises to his feet, takes her hand, and guides her to a spot in the middle of the room, not far from where Trisha and Chas are locked together.

The evening wears on and on. I smooth my dress until my fingers go numb. I sip my Coke until my stomach aches from the sweetness. Trisha and Chas dance their way through song after song after song, blending together until they're as indistinguishable as a candle and its flame. As I look around the room, I know I'll never be as happy as they are in this moment. Not until a head of blond hair appears in the doorway and surveys the tables scattered around the darkened room. His tie is knotted perfectly, his white shirt as crisp as moonlight on a pond. I stand up slowly, reluctant to move in case it's a dream. Vince completes his assessment of the venue and lets his gaze settle on me. A smile unfolds on his lips. He wends his way through the chaos with his hands in his pockets, and finally meets me at the edge of the dance floor.

"Hi," he says brightly.

"Hi," I say back, pushing my hands down the front of my dress one last time.

"I was hoping to get here earlier, but your father needed help with one of the calves." Vince looks me over slowly, appreciating every stitch and bead. "You look… stunning."

"You don't look half bad yourself. Is that one of dad's shirts?"

"No, it's mine. Your mother ironed it for me though."

"How did you get in?" I ask. "I only purchased one ticket."

"Yeah, but I purchased two." Trisha comes up behind me leading Chas by the hand. A thin layer of sweat glistens on her forehead and Chas's boutonniere has a crumpled petal.

Trisha motions to Vince and explains, "After you told me Vince wasn't coming, he and I had a little, shall we say, heart to heart?" She smirks. "I told him that after everything you've done for him, he owes you, at the very *least*, a proper dance. I went back to the ticket table and bought the last one they had."

"She was extremely convincing," Vince admits. "Simply wouldn't take no for an answer."

"Gabby's my best friend, which means she deserves the best." Trisha squeezes my arm and smiles. "Chas and I are going to take a quick breather. You and Vince feel free to take our place."

After Trisha and Chas leave, I'm still trying to process everything she's said. I've never felt like Vince owed me anything—never wanted him to feel like a burden. And he's already done more for me than I could've ever dreamed. I look at the boy in the attic and resist the urge to correct the fit of my dress, knowing Vince will still see the best in me, even if it's not perfect.

As the music favours a slower pace, he extends his hand toward me and asks, "May I have this dance?"

"Define 'dance,'" I reply, buying us a few more seconds of privacy at the edge of the room.

"Three minutes in moderately uncomfortable proximity to other people, with the most beautiful girl in the room."

Fitting my fingers into his, I lead him onto the dance floor. Vince's hands find a home on my waist, pulling me into the warmth of his body. I wrap my arms around his shoulders and rest my head on his chest, hearing every beat of his heart as if it were my own.

"Are you happy, Gabrielle?"

"Yes." I open my eyes. "Are *you* happy?"

"Do you really need to ask?"

"Probably not."

We continue to spin, alone in the crowd with the lights and the music and each other. Round and around we go, and where we stop, only we'll ever know. Don't stop, Vince.

Don't stop.

JESSICA INGOLD is the author of several books for young and new adult readers. With over ten years of experience in writing and self-publishing, her goal is to craft stories that resonate with book enthusiasts of all ages.

Twitter.com/JessieIngold

Instagram.com/author_jessica_ingold

https://authorjessicaingold.wixsite.com/mysite

Other books by Jessica Ingold:

The Moving Mountains series:

Fate Unwritten (#1)

Roads Untraveled (#2)

Words Unspoken (#3)

—

The Spirit Catchers

Captured

—

The Absentees

—

Quiet: Poems about love, loss & healing

Listen: Poems for a noisy planet

www.ingramcontent.com/pod-product-compliance
Lightning Source LLC
Chambersburg PA
CBHW022046050726
47591CB00002B/412